ALSO BY P.

Sweet Dreams, Sweet Death

Everybody loves Chef Garcia's key lime coconut petit fours. Some even say they're to die for. When four guests die at a wedding at the Beaux Rêves Hotel, the famous petit fours are blamed.

Insurance investigator Amy Lynch flies to Key West to prepare for a wrongful death suit. Her investigation is beset with problems. Hotel management pushes for a quick settlement regardless of fault. Local police call it a tragic accident. Potential witnesses are missing, deceased, or unhelpful. Amy fends off pressures from all sides and encounters death everywhere. The health inspector dies in an accident; the local reporter turns up drowned; a homeless woman Amy befriends is found dead. And deceased wildlife crosses her path more than once.

As she forges on in the face of these obstacles, Amy wonders if Key West is the tropical paradise of the travel brochures or a petri dish of death.

"Norton weaves realistic professional procedure and unexpected emotional jolts into the otherwise erotic flavor of Key West, creating a debut that will seriously contend for all the 'Best First' awards."
—Author Jeremiah Healy

"An impressively crafted and unfailingly entertaining novel by a master of the genre, Sweet Dreams, Sweet Death *by P.K. Norton is the first volume in what promises to be a simply out-standing new series starring Amy Lynch, female investigator."*
—James A. Cox
Editor-in-Chief, Midwest Book Review

Dead Drop

Does the past ever really leave us? Not in Amy Lynch's world. What starts out to be a well-deserved vacation for Amy—volunteering at an archaeological dig on the outskirts of Paris—turns ugly when the head archaeologist is found dead at the dig-site. A recently uncovered relic from World War II threatens to expose treachery and betrayal from the time of the German Occupation. It endangers the life of anybody bold enough to delve into its significance.

New England Casualty and Indemnity, the insurance company where Amy works as a claims investigator, is insuring the dig. Amy's world turns upside-down as she reverts from vacation mode to conduct a full-blown investigation. She meets with obstacles, resistance, and threats to her own safety—as well as an adorable French detective—in her quest to unmask a traitor.

"Norton has created an engaging protagonist in Amy, who is bright, brave, and tenacious. The tale features a small cast of characters, as many players disappear shortly after being introduced, so Amy has to carry the narrative load. Fortunately, she's up to the challenge; readers should quickly get involved in what happens to the feisty, heady heroine. With a neat twist in her fast-paced narrative, the author illustrates how events from 80 years in the past can affect people in the present, even Amy herself. Norton seamlessly blends history and mystery into a spellbinding thriller. This sequel accomplishes the unlikely feat of making an insurance investigator enthralling."

—Kirkus Reviews

Deep Secrets

Dead men tell no tales. Is that why Tom Griffin is lying near death in a Cape Cod hospital? Because of what he could reveal about Waltower—a top secret government project underway at Woods Hole Oceanographic Institute?

That's what Amy Lynch aims to learn. As an investigator for New England Casualty and Indemnity, Amy's job is to look into the supposed accident that put Tom into a coma. Amy has a personal stake as well. Tom Griffin is an old friend. Her first love. She struggles to keep her emotions in check as she seeks to discover what really happened to Tom. And why.

Amy fights her way through the sand-bagging she receives from WHOI. They say the project is need-to-know. Well, Amy needs to know. And the clearer the situation becomes to her, the greater the threat to her safety. Will she uncover the truth in time to save herself from the same fate as Tom?

"If you love reading solid mysteries with a heroine you can identify with, then look no further than novelist P.K. Norton. Deep Secrets is her latest installment featuring intrepid insurance investigator Amy Lynch. Amy is no ordinary sleuth and the mystery set in and around Cape Cod will keep you guessing to the end!"
—Jordan Rich, WBZ iHeart Radio

"Norton draws on her experience working in the insurance industry to good effect in this latest series outing ... [she] manages to make insurance-related details as compelling as evidence collection in a conventional murder mystery. The plot is well-paced ... the characters are well-drawn. An entertaining, well-plotted mystery that offers good characterization and unexpected twists and turns."
—Kirkus Reviews

Direct Elimination

There is no such thing as a coincidence. Or is there? Are random occurrences which take place at the same time, or in the same location, totally unrelated events? Or do they converge in time and space in order to right a wrong or put the universe back on track?

In other words, is there a connection between the dead fencer found by firefighters in Andy Yesley's cellar and the 20-year-old baby's skeleton also discovered there?

This is what insurance investigator Amy Lynch must determine as she delves into the fallout from what at first appears to be an ordinary fire loss.

"It's a story that has a tragic beginning and a bittersweet ending. Leave it to Norton, who spent her entire career in the insurance industry, to make investigating claims seem exciting, a formidable task ... This fast-moving mystery injects thrills and sizzle into claims settlement."

—Kirkus Reviews

DEADLY DIAMONDS

An Amy Lynch Investigation

P.K. NORTON

Visit our website at
www.StillwaterPress.com
for more information.

First Stillwater River Publications Edition

ISBN: 978-1-955123-17-4

1 2 3 4 5 6 7 8 9 10
Written by P.K. Norton
Cover design by Emma St. Jean
Published by Stillwater River Publications,
Pawtucket, RI, USA.

Publisher's Cataloging-In-Publication Data
(Prepared by The Donohue Group, Inc.)
Names: Norton, P. K., author.
Title: Deadly diamonds / P.K. Norton.
Description: First Stillwater River Publications edition. |
Pawtucket, RI, USA : Stillwater River Publications, [2021] |
Series: An Amy Lynch investigation
Identifiers: ISBN 9781955123174
Subjects: LCSH: Women insurance investigators--Massachusetts--
Fiction. | Jewelry theft investigation--Massachusetts--Fiction. |
Diamond jewelry--Massachusetts--Fiction. |
LCGFT: Detective and mystery fiction.
Classification: LCC PS3614.O78266 D43 2021 |
DDC 813/.6--dc23

For Tom, whom I killed in Deep Secrets. *The good news is that he is back among the living. It seems you can't keep a good man down—or dead.*

As always, I am forever grateful to my good friends and kind critics Ruth, Kathryn, Toby, Zoe, Jane and Lindsy for their invaluable help. And a special thank-you to Jack, who continues to inspire me even though he is gone now.

Chapter 1

Michael usually enjoyed his job. He relished the gamesman-
ship, the need for stealth when stalking his prey, when
learning their ways before selecting the perfect moment
to pounce. From initial reconnaissance, to formulating a plan of attack,
to the final execution, the entire experience delighted him. The young
ones were his favorite. They were usually nice to look at, not to mention
delightfully unpredictable. Stalking them for days at a time could be full
of surprises. They led eventful lives. And sometimes they put up a good
fight. That was always a nice bonus.

But this particular assignment just didn't do it for him. It was too easy.
There was no real challenge at all. And the challenge was what he relished
most in his chosen career. The thrill of the chase.

His current prey was old. And deadly dull. The same thing day after
day. Walk to work. Never leave the office during the day, not even for
lunch. Return home. Always the most direct route. No stops along the way.
Walk the same few blocks. Take that wretched little dog of hers out every
night at 5:30 and again at 8:30 sharp. A different direction than her route
to work, but again, always the same. Three blocks to the left. About face
and return home. That damn dog even did his business in the same spot
every night, which she quickly cleaned up and disposed of in the trash bin
next to her garage.

He could almost live the woman's life for her!

Yet here he was, conducting his research, his due diligence. There was no point in leaving anything to chance, slim though that chance may be. This job was important to his client, and that was all that mattered. The pay was good and Michael liked to play the horses. Might as well get on with it.

Tonight would be the night. The weather worked in his favor. The sky was clouded over and a soft mist dimmed the effect of the street lights. The air was cool enough to be invigorating, but not uncomfortably cold.

He followed his prey home from work, as he had done for the past several nights, always six or eight feet behind. His soft-soled shoes were silent in her wake. Once she entered her house, he returned to the center of town to retrieve his car. He parked under the street light along her dog-walking route, the light which he had broken that morning. Closing his eyes, he took long, slow, deep breaths to keep his heartrate in check. It didn't pay to get too wound up. That's when mistakes could happen. He reviewed his plan in detail, but, as always, left room for last minute adjustments. A little spontaneity might alleviate this otherwise dull assignment.

8:25. He retrieved the hunting knife from his glove box. The very feel of the knife's grip excited him; it was like greeting an old friend. He unsheathed the knife and placed it in his right jacket pocket. Then he exited the car. He grinned and kept his hand in his pocket, where he could snatch the knife up quickly when the moment was right. Holding fast to the weapon, he walked back toward his prey's house, slowly, quietly, gazing straight ahead. She'd be out any minute now, her and that yippy little mutt. He leaned against a tree in her neighbor's front yard. And waited silently.

He heard her before he saw her, locking her front door and chatting foolishly to her dog. They arrived at the sidewalk and turned to the left.

Maintaining a distance of half a block behind her, he made his way silently up the street. The only sound to be heard was that of her clunky old shoes as they echoed on the sidewalk.

A thought occurred to him. He could follow her until she turned around, then pass her on the sidewalk, just to get a good look at her face. Perhaps he'd even smile and nod as they passed each other in the night. He delighted in that idea. Yes, that would add a touch of spice to this otherwise routine encounter.

She barely acknowledged him as she headed home with the mutt, missing her one and only chance to alter her fate. Too bad. He tightened his grip on the knife in his pocket.

He continued a few feet up the street, then reversed direction and closed the distance between them without a sound. As she reached a small wooded area half a block from her home, he arrived directly behind her. Pulling the knife from his pocket, he grabbed her from behind and slit her throat.

Mission accomplished.

Chapter 2

I knocked on my boss Mark's office door, stuck somewhere between trepidation and hope. Being summoned up to Executive Heaven at New England Casualty and Indemnity the first thing on a Monday morning could go either way. Perhaps I was in for a dressing down for some unknown yet odious offense. Or, on the other hand, perhaps Mark had an intriguing case for me to tackle. If given a choice, I'd take the latter.

An engrossing case would be a pleasant way to begin the week. The job had been rather mundane lately. Plenty of claims, but of the ordinary variety. Nothing that cried out for a thorough investigation. Part of the fun of having my business card read "Amy Lynch, Senior Claims Manager" was the opportunity to delve into the oddball claims myself, the puzzles, the challenges. I loved nothing better than a situation I could sink my teeth into. Or perhaps even my whole heart and soul.

"Come in, Amy. Have a seat." Mark Fisher, CEO of New England Casualty and Indemnity and husband of my best friend Nancy, met me at the door. Looking as dapper as always, he greeted me with a smile. So far, so good.

I did a double-take as I entered Mark's inner sanctum. There sat George, one of our claims supervisors. He was also my nemesis. He didn't like me. I wasn't sure exactly why. He reported to me, but I seemed to be the only person who realized that. Why was he here? And why before me?

"Morning, Amy," George smirked.

I pasted on a smile and tried to make nice. "Hello, George. How was your weekend?"

He smirked again, but didn't answer me.

"Thanks for coming, Amy," Mark said. He lowered himself into a chair behind his oversized mahogany desk, then indicated a chair for me across the desk from him and, sadly, next to George. "Please have a seat."

I sat. "What's happening Mark? Is there something I can do for you?" I crossed my fingers, hoping it would be something fun. And that it wouldn't involve George.

"You can take a look at these loss reports." Mark pushed a stack of computer print-outs across the desk to me. "George brought them to my attention last Friday. I spent the weekend trying to get my head around what I see here. Something odd is going on, and we need to nip it in the bud. Before it affects our bottom line any more than it already has."

I took a moment to scan the reports, zeroing in on the summary on the last page, then said, "So losses are on the increase. And by quite a lot from what I see here."

Mark frowned. "Yes, there has been a significant up-tick over the past several months, and it's increasing exponentially, but only with burglary losses."

"How bad is it?" I asked.

Mark knit his brow. "As of last Friday, up 17% over the average for the last five years."

Yikes! That was cause for serious concern. "Are we dealing with a cat burglar on a crime spree?" I asked. That could add some spice to my life, or complicate it unmercifully.

George decided to answer me. "If so, it's a very odd crime spree. And a rather picky cat burglar. He steals only jewelry. Nothing else. And always high-value stones. Diamonds for the most part."

"So we've got a thief with particularly expensive taste," I said.

My meager attempt at levity was met with silence. I always hated it when that happened. I gave the issue additional thought. Paying those losses would put a major strain on our already tight budget. "Are we talking about a specific geographic area? One of the more exclusive suburbs?"

"Neither," Mark said. "That's what makes no sense. These thefts are scattered state-wide, seemingly at random. There's no large concentration in any particular town, wealthy or otherwise. Whoever our burglar is, he sure gets around."

I digested what I had heard so far, then said, "From what I see in this report, I feel there has to be more than one criminal person involved here. I don't see how a single individual could manage all this without help."

"You're probably right," Mark said. "But for the sake of ease, let's discuss him in the singular. It's simpler that way."

George scowled. I wasn't sure exactly why.

"So, how does he identify which houses to hit?" I asked. "How does he know who has valuable jewelry and who doesn't?"

Mark chewed on his lower lip. "That's an excellent question," he replied. "And it worries me more than I care to admit. We can't allow this to continue."

"Could the thief be working with a particular agent?" I suggested. "Someone new to us, with state-wide locations and no real track record? Or perhaps a long-time agent whose results have been slipping lately? Someone we've placed on the endangered agency list?"

George looked up from the reports and down his nose in my direction. "Nope. For one thing, there are a lot of agencies involved, with no apparent connection to each other. And only one of them has offices state-wide. They're mostly long-time agents, with decent track records, at least until now. But why are you asking all this? Don't you think I would have already considered these questions before bringing the situation to Mark?"

"Just gathering all the facts," I said. *So back off, Georgie Boy.* "Then the real question here is where this thief is getting his, or her, information."

"That's it in a nutshell," Mark said. "And once that source is found, we need to plug the leak fast. Before the situation gets any worse. The trouble is there's simply no discernable pattern with these losses. At least none that we can see so far,"

I mulled that over. "Nevertheless, common sense says that there has got to be some connection among them, some commonality."

"Agreed," Mark said. "We're lucky that George spotted the problem and brought it to my attention when he did."

George beamed at the praise.

I looked away from his smug face. He was obviously missing something here, or Mark wouldn't be asking me to get involved. "So where do I fit in?" I asked Mark. *And what can I do that George can't? Probably a lot of things.*

"I need you to work with George on this," Mark said, without making eye contact with me. He knew all too well how I felt about George. Probably even felt the same way himself.

I stifled a groan. Working closely with George was like having a sour stomach. And that was no secret to Mark.

"We need to put a stop to this situation before New England Casualty and Indemnity is bleeding diamonds," Mark continued. "We can't afford a major increase in losses of any kind right now. You know that. Times are tough."

Was that all he wanted me to do? Just work with a man who disliked me and help him solve a problem he couldn't handle on his own? *Oh joy!*

George scowled in my direction.

Mark started to say something, but George cut him off. "Seems to me the first thing we need to do is fire all the agents who've been experiencing these losses."

Mark winced. "We can't do that, George. You should know that."

"And why not?" George asked.

"Because they don't work for us. They're independent agents who do business with more than one insurance company. Besides that, we have contracts with them. Long term contracts. And up until now, they have always given us very profitable business. Despite this disturbing current trend, we would like that relationship to continue."

I sat and listened to this exchange, appalled at George's misconception of our business model.

George stared at his hands. "Yeah, right. Of course I know that."

Mark turned to me. "The reason I want you to get involved, Amy, is that this investigation will involve contacting, and interviewing, a number of agents. That'll mean lots of time out of the office. Lots of face-to-face contact. More than a little hand-holding as well. The agents respond well to you. That's going to be important here. We don't want to come on too strong and end up needlessly offending somebody. We can't afford to create any ill will."

"Have you considered the idea that the source of information could be internal?" I asked.

Mark's expression darkened. "Unfortunately so. And that's the other reason I need you and your team to be involved. Something tells me you'll come up with a way to investigate that possibility without creating an atmosphere of fear or mistrust among employees. The last thing we need here is a panic among the ranks. We need to approach this issue with tact and discretion. I know I can count on you to make that work."

George's eyes cast virtual daggers in my direction.

"Nothing personal, George," Mark continued. "Your expertise is more in the analytical side of things. You're good at handling data, manipulating it. Amy is more of a people person. I appreciate both of you giving your best efforts to get to the bottom of this."

George glared at me, then asked, "So what, exactly, do we tell the staff as we go about investigating them?"

"Absolutely nothing," Mark told him. "Mum's the word. Even if nobody at NEC&I is involved, if word of this spread around it could generate a panic that the company is in trouble. And we certainly can't afford to have a mass exodus of seasoned employees. Either way, I am confident that Amy will find a way to make it work."

"Right. Sure," George grunted. "Will there be anything else Mark?"

"I believe that covers it." Mark stood, signaling that the meeting was over, then added, "Amy, will you please stick around for a minute?"

Heading for the door, George said, "I guess I'll be on my way to get started analyzing reports and manipulating data." Turning to me, he added, "Good luck Hotshot. Let me know if you need any help."

Mark didn't speak until George was out of ear-shot. "Does he often call you Hotshot?"

I nodded. "Yeah. Most of the time. I choose to take it as a compliment."

"I suppose you might as well." Mark sat back in his chair and stared at the papers on his desk. "What do you know about Natalie Price?" he asked.

"George's assistant? Not much. I don't know her very well." I decided it was best to keep any additional thoughts to myself.

"But ...?" Mark asked. "I know you better than that, Amy. You must have some opinion of her. You usually do. I'd like to hear it."

"As a matter of fact, I consider the woman to be an officious prig," I answered. *He asked for it; he got it.*

Mark laughed. "Come on Amy, don't hold back. Please tell me what you really think." He furrowed his brow. "Actually, I'm not quite sure what an officious prig is, but it doesn't sound too positive."

"It isn't. Why are you asking about her?"

Mark flipped through the computer print-outs on his desk and pulled one page out. "Because George neglected to dispose of the cover sheet that came with this report. It's addressed to Natalie, not George."

Hmmm. "Do you think George needed the data and asked Natalie to request it for him?" I asked, trying to cut the man some slack for a change. Lord knew why, but I was.

Mark gave me a wry smile. "I suppose that's one possibility. Or perhaps she's the one who discovered the trend and requested the reports in the first place. And George is taking credit for her work."

I decided to be honest and open with Mark. "From what I've heard through the grapevine, it wouldn't be the first time he's done that."

"I know. I've heard rumors and innuendos to that effect. Still, I'm sure you'll find a way to work well with him on this. " Mark shrugged. "Anyway, the reason I asked you to stick around is that Nancy wants you and Pete to come to dinner a week from this Saturday."

Nancy was Mark's wife, and my best friend. It was a little weird having him as my boss under the circumstances, but we managed to make it work. Though I definitely enjoyed Mark my friend more than I did Mark my boss. "I'd love to come," I said. "But is Nancy up for this? After all, she gave birth less than two months ago. And I doubt if either of you is getting much sleep."

Mark shook his head. "You're right about that. But we'll get through it. Anyway, Nancy feels she'll be doing all right by then. She wants to discuss plans for the christening with you. Pete and I can watch the hockey play-offs while you two ladies plan the festivities."

"Don't you want any input? At least where the party is concerned?" *And maybe I'd like to watch some hockey, too.*

"Nope. I trust you and Nancy implicitly."

"If you say so. It'll be nice to spend some time with my new godchild. How is my favorite baby?"

"Kevin is doing just fine." Mark beamed. Fatherhood agreed with him.

"I'll check with Pete and see if he's free. In the meantime, it seems I better get working on this case."

I picked up the reports from Mark's desk, then sighed as I walked down the five flights of stairs to my office. Jewelry thefts. Interesting enough, I supposed. I'd been hoping for something more exotic, perhaps involving travel to someplace fun. Oh well, at least this would get me out of the office—and apparently all over Massachusetts. Peggy and Tiffany could handle the internal work while I concentrated on the agents. That thought appealed to me. You never knew what might turn up when on the road.

Chapter 3

My assistant, good friend and occasional dog-sitter Peggy was at her desk in my outer office, her mass of red curls looking even more disheveled than usual. She looked up as I walked in. "So, where have you been hiding for the past half hour?"

"And good morning to you as well. How did you know I was even in yet?"

She pointed to my coat on the coatrack she and I shared.

"Guess I can't put anything over on you," I said. "And to answer your question, I've been up in Executive Heaven meeting with Mark. Listen, can you please get hold of Tiffany? I need to speak with the two of you in my office."

"No problem. Anything new and exciting going on?"

"Maybe." I grinned. "But you'll have to wait until Tiffany gets here to find out what."

She shot me an obviously phony scowl. "Not even a hint?"

"Sorry."

Peggy brushed her unruly red curls from her eyes and picked up the phone.

While I waited for Tiffany to arrive, I called my boyfriend Pete. He had two closings today, one on the law practice he was buying from a retiring lawyer and the other on a house. It was in a tiny little town, or village actually, called Massapoag Junction. The village was a charming spot, and just far enough outside of Boston that it didn't qualify as a suburb. Pete was thrilled with both purchases, eager to leave the big city behind him, along with the job he had come to despise, and settle into life in a small town. Today was also moving day.

I knew how badly Pete wanted this change, and I wanted him to be happy. Still, I wasn't quite sure how I felt about his move. He'd be farther away from me and my East Cambridge apartment. The commute between Cambridge and Massapoag Junction was a bear at rush hour, both morning and afternoon. And small-town life sounded like exile to me. After growing up in a small town on Cape Cod, I had come to love city living. And Cambridge was one hell of a cool city.

Pete answered his phone on the first ring. "Ames, hello. What's happening?"

It was nice to hear him in an upbeat mood. It had been a while since he'd sounded so positive. "How'd the closings go this morning?" I asked.

"Like clock-work. With two attorneys involved in a transaction or two, what could possibly go wrong?"

I bit my tongue. Better not to go there. "Where are you now?"

"At the house. The moving van just arrived. I've got a busy day ahead of me."

"Could you use some help?"

"I'd love some. I was just about to call to see if you wanted to come out here for dinner. Help me christen the house."

"Are you cooking?" I asked. Pete was an excellent cook when he made the effort.

"Sorry. Not this time. I haven't had a chance to buy groceries yet. I thought we could check out the local restaurant scene."

"Good thought. How many restaurants are there in Massapoag Junction?"

"More than you'd expect. There's the coffee shop that does only breakfast and lunch. Also Dino's Pizza and Joe's Diner."

"That's a lot for a town with a population of—what—about 5,000?"

He laughed. "More like 9,000, but I know what you mean. Anyway, I was thinking about a place in Sharon. An Irish restaurant called Café Begorrah. What do you think? Shall we give it a try?"

"With a name like that, who could resist? At least they didn't call it Erin Go Bragh. Is Sam invited?" My scruffy mutt and best friend Sam was particularly fond of Pete.

"Of course. But he'll have to eat at home, and guard the place for us while we go out."

"Sounds good. I'll get away as early as I can, pick up Sam and battle the traffic to your house." *And hate every minute of the trip.*

"Great. See you when you get here." He rang off.

Peggy and Tiffany had arrived while I was on the phone and made themselves comfortable in my two visitors' chairs. Tiffany was all decked out in a navy business suit, apparently working at a more professional appearance. While I appreciated the effort, it wasn't exactly necessary. We tended to be somewhat informal at New England Casualty and Indemnity.

"So," Peggy said, "what's up?"

"We have a mission."

That got Tiffany's attention. "A mission? Please tell me it's a secret one."

I nodded. "It is. At least in part. Still, we're going to need help from a lot of other people. We just need to find a way to get their input without letting them know what is actually going on."

The two of them sat up straight.

"Shall we take notes?" Peggy asked.

"Absolutely. Lots of them."

Peggy stood, grabbed paper and pens for the two of them. "Speak, oh Boss Lady. We are listening."

I took a moment to collect my thoughts. "Over the past several months, NEC&I has had a 17% increase in theft losses."

"Burglaries or robberies?" Peggy asked. She was a stickler for details.

Tiffany gave her an odd look. "Aren't they the same thing?"

"They're both types of theft," I explained, "but robbery is theft directly from a person and usually includes intimidation or threat of bodily harm. Burglary is more by stealth. It involves breaking and entering in order to commit a theft."

"Does it matter which one it is?" Tiffany asked.

Peggy decided to answer that. "It does if you're the victim."

"Well said," I told her, then went on to fill them in on what Mark and George discussed with me.

Tiffany listened with a serious look on her face. "How bad is a 17% increase?"

"Pretty bad," I replied.

"As in, it could possibly put us out of business?"

"Eventually, although we're nowhere near that stage yet. We just need to stop these thefts before we reach that point."

"And the thief only takes jewelry, huh?" she asked.

I nodded. "Mostly diamonds. So we're looking for a jewel thief, or a gang of them, with expensive taste."

Tiffany scrunched up her face for a moment. "And we need to figure out where this thief is getting his information. How he knows where the expensive jewelry is to be found all over the entire state of Massachusetts."

"That's it exactly," I said. The girl was showing a lot of promise as an investigator. She asked a lot of questions, good ones for the most part, and nosy is good in our business.

"What's our plan of attack?" Peggy asked.

"We'll begin by printing out all available information on the ten or twelve agents who are the worst offenders. We'll concentrate on those."

"Stop right there," Peggy interrupted. "Do we need to print them out? Why can't we simply work on line? It'd save a lot of paper."

The technophobe in me grimaced. "Partly because it's easier, and clearer, to make notes on actual paper. Besides, I'll need the printouts to take with me on the road."

Peggy rolled her eyes. "You could always bring your laptop with you."

"And you could always do as I ask." I laughed as I said this, but she appeared to get the point.

"So," I continued, "Tiffany, please take care of those printouts—general information as well as claims history. And try to do it when nobody's watching."

She nodded. "Yes, boss."

I thought for a moment. "Peggy, please contact all the police associated with the losses in question. See if they have any additional information since we received their original reports. Then we'll divide and conquer, each of us according to our own specific skills," I said. "Peggy, you'll run and analyze reports as needed. That's your area of expertise." *And I'd be damned if I'd rely on George's take on the facts.* "We need you to look at the data from every conceivable angle. Concentrate on the dozen or so agencies with the largest numbers of burglary losses. Look for a pattern. Massage the reports until they spew out something useful. Also, you'll need to hold down the fort here, because I'll be out and about visiting the same agents. Picking their brains raw."

Peggy grinned. "So you're on the road again, huh?"

I nodded. "Right. Me and Willie Nelson. It's a tough job, but somebody has to do it."

"How come you always do the road trips?" Peggy teased. "Once again, you get to have all the fun."

I couldn't argue with that. "That's because I'm nice, when I have to be. Or at least I'm diplomatic. We've got to tread lightly with these agents. We can't risk offending any of them."

"Why not?" Tiffany asked. "After all, they do work for us."

I sighed at her lack of understanding of our business model, then realized I couldn't blame the girl. She got her initial training from none other than George himself. It was time for a brief lesson in our corporate structure. "Actually, no, Tiffany. They don't work for us; they work with us. They're independent agents, who do business with NEC&I as well as with a number of other insurance companies. They get to choose where to place their business. We want them to like us. And to give us all their best business. On the other hand, if one of them is up to anything nefarious, we need to know about that as well. And do what we can to stop it."

"Gotcha." Tiffany nodded.

"And I get to stay here and pore over reports." Peggy said, putting a big phony pout on her face.

I laughed. "It is your specialty. You certainly are a nerd at heart."

"I don't apologize for that. I love a good puzzle."

"Where do I fit in?" Tiffany asked.

"You deal with the underwriters who are assigned to the agents who have been experiencing these losses. Interview them. And their assistants as well. Hang out with them in the lunchroom. Eavesdrop on their conversations. Do whatever you can to get the low-down on their agents. If you dig deep enough, maybe you'll see a trend. Something which would make certain agents attractive to a jewel thief. But you need to do it all without letting them know what is actually happening here."

Tiffany gave me a semi-horrified look. "You don't think one of our underwriters is involved in this, do you?"

I flipped through the report Mark had given me. "I certainly hope not, but I suppose anything is possible. The losses are spread all over Massachusetts, though, which would mean there'd have to be more than one underwriter involved. Still, we have to check it out. And, as I said, always without revealing our true mission."

"That could get tricky," she said. "but intriguing at the same time. So basically, you just want me to gossip, right?"

I gave that some thought. "Let's make it a little more official than that. More formal. And entirely untrue. Tell them you're working on a project aimed at improving agency-company relations. That we're looking to reassign agents to different underwriters, to mix things up, and we need to determine the best fits."

"They'll love that," Tiffany said. "A chance to get rid of their difficult agents."

"That's a big part of it, and it's the kind of thing you do well, Tiff. People love to talk and you love to listen. Keep detailed notes and relay the info to Peggy. Between the two of you, I'm sure you'll find something useful."

Tiffany smiled. "Sounds like it will be a nice challenge. Should I be speaking only with the underwriters who deal with the agencies with the most theft losses?"

"No. Talk to all of them, just to cover all bases. And so they'll believe your cover story about possible reassignments. I'll fill Mark in on what you're doing. And who knows? Maybe he'll decide it's a good idea to make a few changes."

"This will be fun," Tiffany said. "Much better than spending my days working with George. Do I still have to do the rest of my job as well?"

I suppressed a laugh. "Of course you do. But this mission gets priority." I gave Peggy the loss data Mark had given me. "Can you please make copies for each of us, highlighting the ten or twelve worst offenders?"

"Will do."

"Then," I continued, "Please call those agents and arrange appointments for me to meet with them over the next few days."

"Sure thing. And I'll do my best to set meetings up in a geographically convenient way. No sense wasting gas. Anything else?"

"Just one thing. Please pull the files on the agencies for the next couple of days, so I can take them with me when I leave today. After that I'll drop by regularly to return them and pick up others."

Peggy rolled her eyes. "Again I ask, why not just take your laptop? The electronic files should provide all the info you'll need." She stopped short of saying I was a technophobe, but I heard it anyway.

"Oh, I intend to do that as well," I said. "But I want to have the paper files as a back-up, or a supplement. You'd be amazed how much additional information you find in them that never makes it into the electronic files."

Tiffany's eyes grew wide. "Really?"

"Maybe," Peggy replied. "Maybe sometimes. But not always."

I chimed in. "Think of it as the difference between receiving a text from somebody and having a face-to-face conversation, Tiffany. It simply works better for me. OK, ladies. Let's get cracking. Before any more expensive jewelry goes missing."

Chapter 4

I loved my Mustang convertible. It was getting older now, but that didn't bother me. It was a classic. And I thoroughly enjoyed driving it—everywhere except in Boston traffic. Today, the rush-hour drive was particularly tough. It took me over an hour to cover the 25 miles between my place in East Cambridge and Pete's new home in Massapoag Junction. I used the time to fill my dog Sam in on my latest case. Good old Sam never said much, but he was a wonderful listener.

The moving van was pulling out of the driveway when we arrived at Pete's. I parked in front of the house—a cute little one-story clapboard cottage with faded blue shutters. The whole place was in need of a fresh coat of paint and the window boxes cried out for something bright and cheerful to be living in them. Pete would get to all that in time. No need to rush.

My favorite part of the property was the yard. There was a small fenced-in area in the back that was perfect for Sam. Beyond the fence, the land sloped gently down to a pretty little pond. That would be nice on summer evenings. And Sam would love watching the ducks.

Pete greeted us in the front yard. "How was your drive?"

"Don't ask," I growled as I opened Sam's door and allowed him to give Pete a proper canine greeting. "Talking about it would only make me cranky."

Pete laughed. "Did you ever consider taking the commuter train?"

"No, I didn't. I didn't think it was an option."

"How come?"

"Because I don't want to leave Sam alone and lonely at home."

"Doesn't Sam like the train?" Pete asked.

"I don't know. I always assumed the train didn't like Sam. And all other potential canine passengers."

"That's where you're mistaken," Pete said. "Dogs are allowed on the commuter rail. And there is a station within walking distance of here."

That came as a surprise to me. A very nice surprise.

I had a surprise for Pete as well. Reaching behind the driver's seat of my Mustang, I pulled out a gift bag. "Happy house-warming."

"Geez, Ames, you didn't have to do this."

"I wanted to."

He reached into the bag and retrieved a 16 x 10-inch wooden plaque suitable for hanging on a front door. He turned it upside-down, on its side and right-side-up, then gave me a quizzical look.

"It says 'welcome' in Ogham," I told him.

"Ohm? What the heck is that? It sounds like something right out of a yoga studio."

"It's an ancient Celtic written language," I told him. "It's spelled OGHAM and pronounced OHM. Gaelic is funny like that. Ogham is carved into large stones all over Ireland. Sort of like runes, or hieroglyphics, except that Ogham writing uses an alphabet rather than pictographs."

"And precisely why am I welcoming people to my new home in ancient Celtic? You do know I'm French Canadian, right?"

"On your father's side. Your mother is of Irish descent."

"Half," he said.

"Right. And I wanted to honor that part of your heritage."

Pete raised his eyebrows. "Thanks. It's a lovely gift." He gave me a quick tour of the house. It was small, but well laid-out, and with plenty of room for no more than two people. Nothing had been unpacked yet, but all the boxes were in the right rooms. He had done a good job arranging what little furniture he owned. He'd figure the rest out in time. Decorating was not my forte, but I'd do what I could to help fill the empty spaces. We left Sam in charge of the house and headed to Sharon for dinner.

In the car, I said, "I'm somewhat surprised to find an Irish restaurant in Sharon. You just don't see that many of them around."

"I can name three of them in Boston right off the top of my head," Pete said.

I considered that a challenge. "Is that so? Well, let's see, there's the Eire Pub in Dorchester."

"And that Irish bakery in Adams Corner," he added. "They serve breakfast and lunch. And there's Amrhein's in South Boston. That's been there forever."

"I stand corrected." *And I hated it when that happened.*

Café Begorrah was in a strip mall a few miles from what passed for a downtown in Sharon. Parking was abundant. We parked the car right by the door and ventured inside. The restaurant was small and simply decorated. Nothing fancy at all. Wooden tables and chairs, painted white and festooned with shamrocks. And it was virtually empty. Maybe the locals didn't dine out on Monday evenings. Maybe they weren't big on Irish cuisine.

A young woman with stereotypic red hair, green eyes and fair skin greeted us at the door. "Good evening, folks. Are you here for dinner?" There was just a trace of a brogue in her voice.

We nodded.

She smiled and surveyed the room. "Sure looks like you've got your choice of tables."

"How about one by the window?" Pete suggested.

Apparently he wanted a view of the parking lot. Oh well. We ordered a bottle of wine, Australian, not Irish, and settled in to peruse the menus.

There was only one other person in the Café Begorrah, an overweight, gray-haired man seated at a table for two by the door to the kitchen, wearing an ugly tweed suit and a sour expression. He was working away at his laptop and barely glanced in our direction. The owner, perhaps? Or simply a solitary diner?

The waitress approached our table. "Do you folks have any questions on the menu?"

"What do you suggest?" I asked.

"I'm partial to the shepherd's pie."

"That works for me," I said.

Pete ordered beef and Guinness stew, then raised his wine glass. "Here's to a new beginning for me. And for us."

"I'll drink to that," I said. It would be nice to see him happy again. He'd been miserable at his old job for ages.

"So, tell me more about this Irish writing. What's its name again?"

"Ogham," I told him. "I learned about it when my parents took me to Ireland after high school graduation. My dad was always a big archaeology buff. We visited lots of fascinating old ruins there, saw Ogham everywhere we went. And I got hooked on digging up the past."

"So that's what convinced you to minor in archaeology in college?"

I nodded.

"Also what brought you to work on that dig in Paris last year. What's next, Egypt?"

"No need for that," I said. "There's plenty of ancient history around New England."

"Such as?"

"Dighton Rock, for one thing. And the old Viking tower in Newport, Rhode Island."

He wrinkled his brow. "Never heard of either of those."

"I'll take you to visit them some time. We'll consider it a field trip."

The waitress brought us a basket of brown bread warm from the oven and some butter. The aroma made my mouth water.

"Enjoy," she said. "Your dinners will be coming out shortly."

The man at the corner table looked up. "Moira, get over here," he growled. He proceeded to give her the devil about something or other—I couldn't hear well enough to know exactly what. She answered him angrily, but again not loudly enough for me to hear what she was saying. Whatever it was, he didn't appear to like it at all. "Talk to me like that again and you'll find yourself in big trouble," he snarled. "Now get out of my sight."

She lowered her head, but didn't respond to him. Then she stomped off to the other side of the room. He returned his attention to his laptop.

Pete and I observed this scene in amazement. What kind of a place was this anyway? If this shouting and bickering was a regular thing, it was no wonder the place was empty. I shuddered, then observed Moira as she sat down and opened a book. She appeared to begin studying something. Oddly enough, the book looked vaguely familiar to me.

I forced the ugly scene from my mind and said to Pete, "How did your day work out? It looks like your move went smoothly."

He nodded. "Pretty much, yeah. I didn't make it to my new office yet, though. That'll happen tomorrow."

"It should be interesting," I said. "This is all such a big step for you."

"And one I'm eager to attack." He pursed his lips. "There was one strange thing, though. Something slightly unsettling."

"Oh?" That took me by surprise. Pete was generally pretty unflappable. Nothing much managed to upset him. "What was that?"

He took a deep breath, then began, "Before the closing this morning, I went to the insurance agency on Main Street where I'd bought my new homeowners policy."

"To get a binder and a paid receipt for the closing," I said. "That's standard procedure. What was unsettling about it?"

"Arlene, the woman who sold me the policy the other day, wasn't there. The other woman in the office told me that she was dead."

Slightly aghast, I waited for the other shoe to drop.

Pete's face darkened. "She was killed in a mugging."

"Killed how?" I had to ask.

Pete grimaced. "Her throat was slit."

Yikes! That was more than unsettling. It was downright frightening. "Oh dear," was about all I could manage to say.

"And it gets worse," he continued. "She was a local woman. Born and bred in Massapoag Junction. She was also the first person I met in town."

"This is disturbing," I said. "Are you sure this town is a safe place to live?" *Or did you perhaps just make one of the biggest mistakes of your life?*

"I certainly hope it's all right." Pete shrugged. "I'm planning to be living here for the long haul."

I shuddered. "Let's talk about something less gruesome. Have you met any of your neighbors yet?"

"I have. The woman next door came over to introduce herself. Her name's Martha Randall. She's very chatty. She's also the person who suggested this restaurant."

"Might I have some competition from her?" I teased.

"Not likely. She appears to be older than my mother." He took a sip of wine.

My eyes settled on the wall behind him. Two framed photos hung there, both of men who looked vaguely familiar. "Take a look at those pictures," I said, pointing. "Do you know who those men are?"

Pete turned and stared for a moment. "Eamon DeValera on the left. You know, a former president of Ireland. And that's Whitey Bulger on the right."

Whitey Bulger? "DeValera I can understand. That makes some sense in an Irish restaurant. But Whitey Bulger? Good grief, Pete what do you suppose is up with that? I mean really, Whitey was pretty much the ultimate bad guy. Why would anybody want to hang a picture of him?"

"Damned if I know," Pete shrugged. "Maybe it was the only other well-known Irishman they could think of. I can't say it adds much to the atmosphere of this place though."

"I think it makes it a little creepy. Not to mention that we're the only customers here. Why do you suppose that is?"

He shook his head. "Perhaps because it's a Monday evening, and on the early side for dinner. Or perhaps it has only recently open and word hasn't spread about it yet."

"You're probably right. Still, it seems off to me."

"Did anybody ever tell you your job is making you overly suspicious? You tend to see crimes and misdemeanors everywhere."

"Maybe so. Or maybe I'm simply better tuned in to what's going on around me."

He squeezed my hand. "So, tell me about your day."

I gave him a brief overview of my current mission.

"A jewel thief huh? That could be intriguing."

"I agree. And it will get me out of the office. Peggy has already set up appointments for me for the next several days."

He smiled. "Being on the road is always a plus for you, isn't it? Any thoughts on how you're going to attack this case?"

"Sort of." I admitted. "Common sense says there has to be some connectivity here. I merely have to find it."

"Is that all?" Pete laughed. "Well, it sounds like a good challenge. And I'm available to assist you as needed."

That was a nice thought, but he'd probably be better off devoting his time and energy to the law practice he had just purchased. I decided to keep this thought to myself. The waitress arrived with our dinners. "Here you go, folks. It sure smells heavenly."

No question about that. I did, however, have a few questions for the girl.

"Is this place new?" I asked.

She shook her head. "No. It's been here forever."

I was tempted to ask if it had always been this empty, but decided to let that slide. I'd already made my point with Pete. Time to change the subject. "What did I see you studying over there?"

"Insurance 101. I'm taking a course." She grimaced. "Boring."

No wonder the book had looked familiar to me. "So you're looking to change careers?"

"I've no choice. Working here is hardly what you'd call a career." She glanced around the room. "Tips tend to be a bit light." She flashed us a smile stuck somewhere between friendly and rather sad.

I could see what she meant. "But why insurance?" I asked. "Particularly since you find it so boring?"

"That's a long story. The simple answer is that I have to do something. I can't continue working this closely with Mr. Personality over there—or I may end up having to hurt the man. Being new to this country makes it all the more difficult. I don't know many people here. Insurance is what is available at this time. I have to take what's offered to me. And boring though it may be, at least it'll pay better." She sighed as she walked away. "Enjoy your meals."

Pete and I were silent as we dug into our respective meals. Warm and hearty, and quite tasty.

"So where will your investigation begin?" Pete asked.

"Fall River," I told him. "I'm heading there first thing tomorrow. Wish me luck."

He smiled. "I always do."

We finished our dinner in comfortable silence. Pete seemed exhausted from his day. I was distracted by my new case, and the mildly toxic atmosphere of the Café Begorrah was only making it worse. Between the obvious animosity we had witnessed and the fact that Pete's insurance agent had been murdered, I was beginning to develop an uneasy sense of foreboding.

Chapter 5

I left Pete's new home first thing in the morning and headed toward the south coast of Massachusetts. Sam was spending the day with Pete, happy to have a fenced-in yard all his own and at least a dozen ducks to observe from a distance. The forecast was for off-and-on rain all day. Not an ideal day for a road trip, but at least I wasn't sitting in Boston traffic. The drive from Massapoag Junction to Fall River was light-years more pleasant than it would have been from Boston in any kind of weather. I began to think there might actually be some benefits to living outside of the big city. I'd think about that later. In the meantime, I made the trip in good time.

Fall River was an old city, dating back to the early 1800s. It was best known for Lizzie Borden, Portuguese culture, re-purposed 19th century textile mills and the world's largest collection of WWII naval vessels at Battleship Cove. None of these was on my agenda today. I had an appointment with Thomas Foye.

The T. X. Foye Insurance Agency had been doing business with New England Casualty and Indemnity for over 22 years. According to the file notes, their results over time had been on the average side—with some good years followed by a few that were not so good—but never anything alarming. Then, about ten months ago, their burglary losses spiked. I needed to discover why.

The agency was located in a tidy little store-front smack in the middle of a slightly shabby business block on Main Street in Fall River. Parking was an issue. I eventually snagged a spot four blocks away and eased my Mustang into it. Parallel parking was always somewhat of a challenge for me. I fed the meter and walked back to the Foye Agency in the rain.

A fellow I assumed to be Thomas X. Foye stood in the doorway checking his watch. He was short and chubby, with gray hair and the map of Ireland on his face.

I turned on my official business smile. "Hello, Mr. Foye. I'm Amy Lynch from New England Casualty and Indemnity."

"Good morning, Ms. Lynch. You're right on time."

He shook my proffered hand. His was clammy.

"Please, come in," he said.

I followed him into a sun-lit room which appeared to be the main office. It was devoid of all decoration. Not even a calendar on the wall. There were two utilitarian desks and chairs, some old file cabinets and very little else. No clutter whatsoever. No piles of files or other paperwork. The only computer in the room appeared to be turned off. Perhaps it was a slow day.

A middle-aged woman stood as we entered. She was tall, thin and over-dressed for the neighborhood, with dark eyes and a headful of auburn curls.

"This is Patti," Foye told me. "My girl Friday. Don't know what I'd do without her." He gave Patti a big toothy smile.

Patti nodded in my general direction. "Morning."

"Why don't you and I step into my private office?" Foye suggested to me. "We'd be more comfortable chatting in there."

"That may not be a good idea," Patti said. "Don't forget that Meghan is out today. Taking a personal day, whatever that means. And she left a nasty pile of notes and problems for me to deal with. I may need your help with those, or if a client comes in while I'm on the phone or busy helping someone else." She frowned ever so slightly at her boss.

It made me wonder who was actually in charge.

Foye shrugged and headed into his office. "Right. Thanks for reminding me. I won't be far away. Just call me if you need me. This way, please, Ms. Lynch. And, by the way, please call me Tom."

I did not suggest that he call me Amy. I preferred not to be on a first name basis with the man, at least until I had a better feel for what was going on.

Foye plopped himself behind his desk and indicated a visitor's chair for me. "You'll have to excuse Patti. She appears to be having one of her cranky days. That tends to happen whenever we're short-handed."

"Stress can do that," I said. Apparently, it had the same effect on him. I couldn't help but notice the nervous tic in his right eye.

"At least Patti's always pleasant on the phone or with walk-in clients," Foye continued. "Thank the good lord. Service with a smile no matter what."

Apparently claims investigators didn't merit that service as well. Was it something I said? Or something I did?

I held my tongue, though not without difficulty and waited for Foye to continue.

He squirmed in his chair, then finally said, "So, what can I do for you today? It's not all that often we get visitors from New England Casualty and Indemnity. I hope there aren't any problems. I value my relationship with your company. Can't go having anything upset the status quo."

I wasn't quite sure what the status quo was. Maybe it needed upsetting. "As my assistant told you when she phoned yesterday, we're looking into theft losses that have occurred over the past year or so," I said. "Jewelry thefts. Mostly diamonds."

Foye furrowed his brow. "So I understand. I wish I knew what to tell you."

"Were you able to pull the files my assistant asked you to look at?"

He raised his eyebrows toward Patti, who had just appeared in the doorway and was not even being subtle about the fact that she was listening in on our conversation.

Patti shook her head. "I didn't get to it. Only got the request yesterday afternoon, you know. And we had a steady stream of walk-in customers yesterday, mostly folks making payments. I couldn't ignore them, you know, when they were coming in to give us money. Then I couldn't stay late to pull the files. Already had other plans."

Some people would have added 'sorry' at that point. Patti chose not to.

"These things happen," I said, struggling to be understanding. "I don't mind waiting while you pull them now. And I'll need the underwriting files as well as the claims information. Basically everything you've got on the clients in question."

Patti looked at me as if she wasn't used to being told what to do. "Coming right up," she said as she strutted off. "Tom, you'll have to mind the phones."

Foye gave me a weak smile. "Patti has been here longer than I have. She worked for my father for years. He passed away suddenly eighteen months ago and I took over the business. I kept Patti on when I came on board because she knew the clients—easier transition, don't you know. At first I needed her, relied on her. That was a big mistake. Now she seems to think she's my boss."

He sat back in his chair and stared at the wall behind me. "So, tell me, is there some sort of problem with these claims you're asking about?" he asked. "Please tell me we're not in any kind of trouble."

"We don't know," I said. "We're naturally curious about the sharp increase in jewelry thefts, but I'm hopeful there's a good explanation. At the moment, we're just gathering information."

Foye stared at his hands. "I don't know how much help I can be to you. Patti generally handles the claims. I concentrate more on sales. Got to bring in new business, you know. I guess I didn't realize that theft losses were up." His voice quavered as he said this, making me wonder if he was being honest with me.

"But you must have seen the trend in your monthly profit and loss statements," I said.

He shook his head. "Come to think of it, I don't remember seeing one of those in a while now. Guess I've been too busy writing new business to notice."

I had trouble believing that but chose not to challenge him. At least not at the moment.

Patti re-appeared at the door with a stack of files in her arms. "Here you go," she said as she dumped them on the desk.

"I understand you're the person who generally handles the claims here?" I said to her.

"Right. Meghan usually deals with the other clerical work, but we back each other up when necessary."

Things seemed to be quiet for the moment in the outer office. I jumped on the opportunity to pick Patti's brain. "Have you noticed anything in particular with the recent theft claims? Maybe something odd, or unusual?"

Patti shrugged. "Seems to be more of them these days, but that comes as no surprise."

"What makes you say that?"

"Crime is up in general around here," she said. "Fall River has changed a lot in the past few years. More folks moving in. Fewer jobs available for them. More and more homeless people. That's bound to lead to a rise in burglaries."

I wasn't so sure about that. A rise in muggings would seem more likely.

Foye cleared his throat. "Is that your phone I hear out there, Patti?"

Patti harrumphed toward the outer office.

I began thumbing through the files. They were neat and well-organized, and very thin.

Foye remained at his desk, not even trying to disguise the fact that he was watching my every move. And with a terrified look in his eyes. I couldn't decide if he was afraid of me or worried about what I might find in the files.

"Is this increase in thefts particular to my agency?" he asked.

I shook my head. "No. Not at all. We're seeing more and more jewelry thefts state-wide."

"Well, there you go then," he said. "So there's nothing wrong here. We're victims, the same as you."

That struck me as a novel take on things. I waited to see if he had anything to add. No such luck.

A phone rang in the outer office. A bell jingled at the same time, as somebody—most likely a client—came in the front door.

Patti called out. "Tom! I could use your help out here."

"I'm OK working alone here if you have something else you need to do," I told him, preferring to study the files without him looking over my shoulder.

"Yeah, right. I'm coming". He turned to me, "Sorry."

I scanned the files one by one but found nothing untoward, or even mildly unusual anywhere—applications, copies of down payment checks, hand-written notes from clients, appraisals from local jewelers, standard claim report forms. Oh well, it was worth the effort if only to convince these folks that I meant business. Though I would have preferred it if I'd found something of interest.

Foye returned a while later and sat back at his desk. "How's it going?"

"Fine. Thanks. I'm just about done. I'll leave these files with you. I'd appreciate it if you could look them over as well within the next few days. To see if you notice anything unusual. Or anything these clients may have in common."

He gave me a weary smile. "I'll do my best, Ms. Lynch. I don't want any trouble here. My contract with NEC&I is important to me. I need to make sure I don't lose it. But it's like I said, Patti knows the clients far better than I do. If they had anything in common, she's the one who'd know. I'll try to discuss these losses with her and get back to you by the end of the week. I am truly sorry I can't be more helpful."

I was sorry too, but needed to keep things positive. "Maybe you'll come up with something I missed. It's worth a try. It doesn't appear to be a good time for me to question Patti. Could you please discuss these losses with both her and ... the lady who isn't here today?"

"Meghan," he said. "Yes, I will surely do that. You have my word."

I hoped he'd keep his word. It was time for me to move on. While I didn't want to let this guy off the hook too easily, there was no point wasting my time this early in the game. I'd get back to him later in the week. Perhaps it would be good for him to worry and stew for a couple of days. And it was painfully obvious that he was already worrying and stewing. The question was: why?

He stood.

Apparently, that was my cue to leave, despite having learned absolutely nothing. I took the hint anyway, thanked him for his time and headed to my car, frustrated with my day so far. Tom Foye struck me as a nice enough guy, but rather clueless, as well as uneasy. And my guess was that Patti ran the office while Tom Foye did whatever it was that he did. I questioned his remark about bringing in new business. According to my files, there hadn't been any noticeable growth in the Foye Agency in ages. It worried me that he didn't have a handle on his monthly profit and loss statements. Maybe that's what happens when you inherit a business. Was the man simply riding on his father's coattails? Maybe he had always hoped for a different career path, but felt he had no real choice but to take over the business.

Did that help to explain what was causing the severe increase in jewel thefts here?

My overall impression of these folks was that neither one of them was being entirely honest with me. I'd figure out why eventually. In the meantime, I hoped my next appointment would be more productive.

Chapter 6

I left Fall River and jumped onto the road to Falmouth, determined not to let this less-than-stellar beginning get me down. It was always easy to be hopeful on the other side of the Bourne Bridge. Simply being on Cape Cod had a wonderful way of elevating my mood and lowering my blood pressure. I smiled to myself as I hit the gas.

I opted for a leisurely drive down Main Street in Falmouth. This made for a slightly longer route to my appointment in East Falmouth, but it was worth the extra time. Falmouth had one of the nicest downtown areas anywhere. There were lots of great little shops, restaurants and art galleries. No time to check them out today though. Sometimes the job has to come first.

The Almeida Insurance Agency was on Route 28 in East Falmouth. NEC&I had done business with them for years. The file referred to it as a solid family business, father and son working well together. I needed to learn what had happened to change that.

The office was located in a lovely little Cape Cod cottage with weathered shingles typical of the area. An identical building next door was home to an attorney's office. I left my Mustang in their shared parking lot and headed in to meet Jose Almeida.

A perky blonde looked up as I came through the door. Her sweater was a bit too tight, her skirt a bit too short, her heels a bit too high. And she was young enough to make that look work for her. Her left thigh sported a small green tattoo of indeterminate design. I decided not to examine it closely.

"Good morning," she said. "What can we do for you today?"

"I'm here to see Jose Almeida," I said, handing her my card.

"I'll let him know." She turned and headed toward the inner office. I looked around. The outer room was small and cozy. Two old-fashioned wooden desks faced the front windows, each holding a computer, an over-flowing "in" box, and a stack of manila folders ready to topple over. Tall gray file cabinets occupied every available inch of wall space. At a glance, it appeared they relied more heavily on paper files than the computer system. People after my own heart, technophobe that I am.

A middle-aged woman who could only be described as frumpy sat at a desk staring at a computer screen but not touching either the mouse or the keyboard. She looked up. "Too bad about the rain today, isn't it? Although I'm sure the lawns need it badly. At least it looks like we might have an early spring this year."

"Let's hope so," I replied.

"I understand you're here to talk about our claims?" she continued.

"That's right. You have had a rather large increase in theft losses this year."

She pursed her lips. "So it seems. But at least they're only theft losses. Nobody gets hurt. Auto accidents would be so much worse. I'd hate to see them increasing as well."

Before I could follow up on that remark, Jose Almeida appeared from the inner office. He was an older man with a slope to his shoulders and a world-weary look in his eyes. "Good morning, Ms. Lynch. It's nice to meet you." He reached out to shake my hand. "Please, meet my staff," he said. He pointed to the woman with whom I had been speaking. "This lovely lady is my daughter-in-law Maria."

Maria, smiled. "How do you do?"

"And this is Sheila," Jose continued. "The latest addition to my staff." The younger woman nodded in my direction.

"Nice to meet you both," I said.

"Please come into my office, Ms. Lynch."

I did as requested. His office was poorly lit, his desk cluttered and dusty.

"Make yourself comfortable," Jose said, steering me toward an uncomfortable-looking wooden chair. He eyed me warily. "We don't get many visits from you folks at NEC&I. I've got a feeling you haven't come here bearing good news."

"What makes you think that?"

"The lady who called to make this appointment for you said you wanted to talk about jewelry thefts."

"That's correct." I waited to see where he would go with this conversation.

He exhaled audibly. "Please tell me we're not in any trouble. I mean, it's important to me to keep you folks happy. To continue to have a good relationship with you. I don't want there to be any problems between us." He shook his head. "I only have one other company, you know."

"How are your loss results with them?" I asked

"The last time I checked, about the same as with you folks at NEC&I."

I wondered how long ago that last time was. "Not to worry, Mr. Almeida. We're trying to get a handle on jewelry thefts over the past year, and hoping your experience might shed some light on what's going on in the area."

He knitted his brow. "Jewelry thefts, huh? Now that you mention it, I guess we have had a few good-sized losses lately."

It was more like a dozen large thefts, which was way out of proportion for an agency of his size. I chose not to point this out to him. Better to keep our conversation friendly, at least for the moment.

"I don't know how much help I can be," he said. "I pulled the files you were interested in. Haven't had much chance to look them over yet though. But I've got to tell you, I was surprised to learn so many of our clients had expensive jewelry. My customers tend to be simple, everyday folks that I've insured for years. A lot of them are relatives, or old friends. I know for sure they're not wealthy. My son always handled most of the new business. Maybe that's where the fancy jewelry coverage came in." A dark cloud passed over his face. "I'm sorry. I meant to say my late son. He passed away a little over a year ago."

"Then I'm the one who's sorry," I said. "A parent should never have to bury a child."

"Amen to that." He frowned. "I'm guessing I'm not the only agent in these parts who is experiencing theft losses."

"What makes you say that?"

"It's the time we're living in. The Cape isn't what it used to be. There's more crime in general. More homeless people. More drugs. The drugs are the real problem, you know. People are stealing anything and everything to buy them. And it's getting worse all the time."

I took note of what he said, but wasn't convinced that was the issue. People with drug problems tended to steal things they could sell quickly, not high-end jewelry. Besides, Jose Almeida's losses were worse than several of our other, larger Cape agents. His theory simply didn't add up.

"Drugs will be the death of us all," he continued. "I can't prove it, but I'm convinced that's what caused my son Eddie's death. He was forced off the road and hit a tree. Witnesses said the other car was going like a bat out of Hell. The driver had to be high on something. The police never did catch the bastard."

That explained his daughter-in-law's comment about thefts being better than crashes. I commiserated with him for a few minutes, and meant every bit of it. "With your son gone, who handles the new business here now?" I asked.

He shook his head. "I'd love to tell you I do, but that would be a lie. Since Eddie's death, I haven't had the heart to do much of anything around here. I built this agency for him. It doesn't matter so much anymore. I only keep it going for Maria and the kids. Gotta make sure they'll be all right."

"It must be very hard for you. So your employees deal with new clients then?"

"That's mostly Sheila. Maria's more the one to provide other services— adding drivers when our clients' kids get their licenses, taking payments, filing claims, things like that. She's having a difficult time since Eddie died. I pretty much let her do whatever she wants around here. Anything to make her happy."

That was a sweet thought, but not necessarily a good business practice.

"Now Sheila," he continued, "she's something else. A real go-getter. Always looking for ways to attract new clients, or sell more coverage to existing ones. All without being the least bit pushy. She has a knack for it, just like Eddie did. I'm lucky to have her on board."

I liked Jose Almeida. He was a sweet, sad, old guy. But he obviously wasn't going to provide me with much useful information. I hoped the ladies in the office would be more helpful. "I'd like to speak with Maria and Sheila now," I said to him.

He stood. "No problem." He headed toward the outer office.

I followed, and quickly learned that questioning these ladies was going to be a problem. Maria was nowhere to be seen and Sheila was on the phone.

"Where's Maria?" Jose asked Sheila.

"Can you please hold on a minute?" she said into the phone, then turned to Jose. "She just left for a doctor's appointment. Remember she told us about that yesterday?" Sheila returned to her call.

"Oh, yeah, right. Sorry, Ms. Lynch."

The front door opened and a young couple stepped into the office.

"What can I do for you folks?" Jose asked.

The man replied, "We're here to see Sheila. She's taking care of the insurance for the summer home we're buying. We're supposed to pick up a binder and a paid receipt."

"Please, have a seat," Jose told them. "She will be right with you."

"Would you mind if I took a look at those files you pulled?" I asked Jose.

"Sure. Come on back to my office."

A few of the files were obviously new clients. Not a lot in the folders. Everything neat and organized. The others were old and bursting with random papers—applications, hand-written correspondence, stray post-it notes. Sadly, nothing which jumped out at me. All evidence of a friendly local business, but nothing of interest.

Sheila was still busy with clients when I finished. I didn't have the time to hang around until she was free. "Can you make some time to look over the files in question?" I asked Jose. "Then discuss them with Maria and Sheila. Maybe they'll be aware of something I missed. Something those clients may have in common, perhaps."

He furrowed his brow. "The only thing I can think of that these folks have in common is that, for the most part, they're all Portuguese. I doubt if that's very helpful. Perhaps Maria or Sheila may see something I'm missing."

"We'd appreciate any thoughts they may have. I'll call you in a couple of days to see if you've come up with anything that might help." Maybe giving him a deadline would spur him into action.

"Will do. So you're not going to cancel my contract with NEC&I?" Jose asked.

I shook my head. "No. We want to work with you to get to the bottom of this. So we can continue to have a profitable relationship." I knew that sounded like a line from the Book of Corporate Hooey, but I said it anyway. Jose Almeida didn't question it. He just looked relieved.

I sat in my Mustang and thought about Jose and Maria Almeida. Could dealing with the death of Jose's son, aka Maria's husband, explain the dramatic increase in their losses? And, if so, how?

I made a note to follow up with both Tom Foye and Jose later in the week. Neither one of them seemed to have a real handle on the goings-on in their offices. That was a concern I'd need to address with Mark. But that would have to wait. My investigation into the jewelry thefts was my main concern at the moment. And I'd pretty much struck out twice so far today. I hoped that my next appointment would prove to be more productive.

My phone dinged to let me know I had a voicemail. "Ms. Lynch, hello. Tom Foye here." That was a surprise. I was pretty sure I had spoken with the man a mere few hours ago. "Listen," the message continued, "whatever you do, don't call me back. That would be too dangerous. You and I need to talk—but it's got to be in private. This is important. And I don't dare say much over the phone. I'll call you back once I figure out where we can get together, and when. Sorry to sound so mysterious, but I don't know what else to do."

Chapter 7

Holy *shit!* What was that all about? Foye sounded frightened. The first question was: of what? And the second one was: why in hell did he bother to call to tell me he couldn't tell me something? I drove off toward my next stop caught somewhere between being curious to hear what Foye needed to discuss and being downright annoyed at the man for leaving me in suspense. Also for getting me so rattled that I didn't think to call Peggy before taking off. I was no good at using my phone while driving and I needed to speak with my assistant. Fast.

I ran into some road work on Route 28. I used the time spent sitting still to call Peggy—hands free, of course. There were cops working a detail for the construction.

"What's happening?" she asked. "Is the weather any better on the Cape than it is here?"

"Unfortunately not," I told her.

"That's a shame."

"As a matter of fact, it's fine with me. A chilly, damp day on Cape Cod beats a warm sunny day in the office any time."

"You're right about that. So what can I do for you?" she asked.

"For the moment, just listen. I need to think out loud. The damndest thing just happened to me. I don't know what to make of it." I gave her a brief summary of my meeting with Tom Foye and his follow-up phone message. "I mean, really, what was the point of calling me at all?"

"Good question. Maybe just to put you on notice that he had some information for you?"

"Then why not just give me the damn information?"

"Beats me. But I'm sure we can figure it out. So what's our next move?"

"The next move is yours," I told her. "And please get Tiffany involved as well. Find out everything you can about Tom Foye, Patti, whose last name I don't know, and anything or anybody else related to that agency. See what you can learn online and from our files. Talk to the underwriters. And do anything else you can think of. I want to be well-informed the next time I speak with Foye."

Peggy laughed. "Not to worry. If I have anything to say about it, you'll be armed for bear."

"Sounds good to me." I hesitated to bring up my next request, not wanting to overburden Peggy.

"Your momentary silence tells me there's something else," she said. "Let's have it."

"I just left the Almeida Agency in Falmouth, having learned next to nothing there either. Can you please take a look at the records for jewelry losses for both these agencies? Check the policy histories. When was the coverage written? Are there any prior losses for those clients? Other policy activity? You know what to look for."

"I do indeed," Peggy said. "I'll get right on it. My only question is which of these two missions is the priority?"

"In a way, they both are, although if I had to choose, I'd put Tom Foye first. Listen, I know I'm asking a lot of you here. If it gets to be too much, please let me know. I'd hate like the devil to push you over the edge."

"I'm a long way from the edge yet," she said. "And Tiffany is a wonderful help. Oh, and speaking of her, you'll be pleased to know that she is happily chatting away with everybody in the lunchroom, and George has steam coming out of his ears."

I laughed. "That is good news. I'm sure she'll manage to pick up a few juicy tidbits. Just ask her to zero in on Foye and Almeida for the moment."

"You've got it," she said. "And, listen, I can tell you're worried about Tom Foye's call, but try to push it out of your mind for the moment. Don't let it interfere with the rest of your mission."

"My plan exactly. Talk to you soon." The traffic began moving just as I ended the call.

Peggy was right, of course. As disturbing as Tom Foye's message was, I couldn't let that distract me. I needed my next agency visit to be productive. I'd already struck out twice today, and it was barely the middle of the day. Ever hopeful, I forged on.

Chapter 8

The construction delay slowed me down just long enough that I wouldn't have time to grab lunch. Bummer. Hunger always made me cranky. Nothing I could do about it though. I cleared my mind, sucked it up and continued down Route 28.

My next stop, the Harlow Insurance Agency, was in Cotuit, a small, well-to-do village halfway between Falmouth and Hyannis. The place had somehow managed to strike the perfect balance between well-heeled and quaint. The local real estate tended to be expensive. The village center was small and charming, featuring a coffee shop, one other restaurant, a post office, a church and a few assorted businesses. Sort of a classier version of Massapoag Junction.

From what I knew about the Harlow Agency, they were a high-end business in a well-to-do locale. Their losses with NEC&I had always been slightly higher than expected, but never quite bad enough to reconsider our contract with them. At least not until lately.

I parked on the street and headed toward the Harlow office. It was in a newer building, painted shiny white. It had lots of windows and extremely well-groomed shrubbery. I checked the time as I walked past the coffee shop. Too late to stop. Francis Harlow was expecting me. The best I could hope for was that my stomach would refrain from growling while I met with him. Finding a cough drop in my purse, I popped it into my mouth. That would have to do for now.

I entered the office to find a man pacing back and forth while speaking loudly on the phone. His navy-blue three-piece pinstripe suit struck me as slightly over the top for Cape Cod, but what did I know? Gentlemen's fashion was never my forte. Unfortunately, he had been way too liberal with his cologne.

The man, presumably Francis Harlow, acknowledged my presence, held up two fingers and walked into the next room. I supposed that meant he'd be with me shortly. I examined the office while I waited. The furniture was sleek and modern. A single desk, currently unoccupied, contained a telephone, the latest in computer equipment—in deep sleep mode—and very little else. There were no file cabinets in sight. The other side of the room was set up for a comfortable tête-a-tête, with a low table surrounded by a couple of chairs.

An attractive young blonde woman emerged from a room in the rear. She was stylish in a cheap sort of way, and showing a lot of cleavage. I may have spotted a small tattoo on her chest. They certainly were the fashion lately. Or perhaps it was just a mole. I decided it would be rude to look too closely. She smiled at me, glared in the man's direction and said, "Sorry about that. I'm sure he'll be available shortly. In the meantime, perhaps there's something I can do for you. By the way, I'm Irina." She pointed to the nameplate on her desk. "Irina Casey."

"Nice to meet you. I'm Amy Lynch from New England Casualty and Indemnity." I gave her my card.

"Right," she said as she studied it. "We've been expecting you. Is there anything in particular you want to discuss, or is this just a social visit?"

"I'm interested in the recent jewelry thefts we've seen from your office."

Irina nodded. "I guess we have had a few lately. Handled the claims myself. His Nibs is far too busy being important to be bothered with such ordinary tasks."

"Is there anything in particular you can think of, anything odd, about these thefts? Or perhaps something they may have in common?"

She shrugged. "Couldn't say. Sorry. I haven't been here long enough to know how things usually work."

"Oh? How long have you been here?" I asked.

"I started exactly ten months and five days ago. Right after I got married. Patrick, that's my husband, got transferred to the Cape so we moved here. I have to tell you, though, I much preferred life in South Boston. People are so much more friendly there."

"What does your husband do?" I asked. Might as well make idle chit-chat while waiting. You never knew what you might learn.

"He's in construction."

I figured he must work for a large construction business to be trans-ferred like that. Most of the companies on the Cape tended to be small and local.

"Have you handled many theft losses in that time?" I asked.

"I have." She said. "And I've got to tell you, people around here can become pretty unpleasant when their lives don't go according to plan. They're rich and spoiled and downright nasty. As if it was my fault some-body made off with their precious jewels."

Before I could pursue this subject, Francis Harlow, aka "His Nibs," re-entered the room.

"How do you do?" He consulted the calendar on his phone. "You must be Ms. Lynch. Please sit down. I can give you about twenty minutes before I have to leave for an important appointment."

Funny. I thought I was his appointment. And I knew I was important. I had hoped for a warmer welcome here, not to mention a longer visit. After all, the man knew I was coming, as well as when. It seemed he didn't want to spend much time with me. I couldn't help but wonder why.

Harlow turned to Irina. "This would be a good time for you to grab some lunch and go to the post office. And hurry back. I have to leave shortly."

Irina scowled, but didn't protest. "Right. Sure. See you shortly." She grabbed a small stack of envelopes from her desk and started toward the door.

"Hold on a minute," Harlow snapped as he eyed the envelopes, then snatched up the one on top. "What the hell is this? Who's this Mullins Brothers Services? We don't deal with anybody by that name. Are you paying your own bills with my postage? Don't you ever let me catch you doing anything like that again."

Irina stood silently as he ranted. Then off she went.

Harlow turned back to me with a big phony smile. The man had far too many teeth. "Now, where were we?" He lowered himself into a chair and indicated for me to do the same. "So what's this about wanting to discuss jewelry thefts? Is there some kind of problem?"

"That's what we're trying to learn," I said, forcing a tight smile. "There's been an upsurge in losses involving expensive jewelry."

"In this office?" He broke in before I could finish my thought.

"Among others."

"So why am I being singled out?"

"I beg your pardon?"

"You heard me. Why pick on my agency if there are others in the same situation?"

I took a long slow deep breath in an effort to control my temper. "Nobody is being singled out, Mr. Harlow. We're touching base with all of our agents who have had significant jewelry losses over the past year or so."

He glared at me. "So now my losses are significant, are they? Well, let me tell you something. My clients are well-to-do. They have expensive jewelry. That's what wealthy people do. They spend their money on nice things. And thieves don't go after the average schmucks. They concentrate their efforts where they can get the biggest return. It makes sense to me." He paused for a moment to study his manicured nails. "Besides, isn't that what insurance is for?"

With an attitude like that, Francis Harlow wouldn't last long in this business. This conversation wasn't going quite the way I had hoped. I wracked my brains to find a different approach. "I'm sure you know that insurance premiums are established by estimating expected losses based on prior loss statistics. Heavy losses over an extended period of time will eventually result in premium increases. People don't like that. Also, agent bonuses are based on loss results which are better than expected." Perhaps I could appeal to his greedy side. "We want to ensure that your bonuses continue."

"Or increase," he said.

Apparently I had found his hot button. "Did you have a chance to look over the losses my assistant mentioned when she phoned you?" I asked.

He nodded. "Checked them out this morning. In great detail, I might add."

"Did you notice anything that the clients involved might have in common? Something that might connect these thefts?"

"The only thing my clients have in common," he said, "is that they're all rich. And I don't know what the big fuss is. In every case, not much was stolen. Just one or two jewelry items. As I said, these are wealthy people. They have a lot of stuff. Probably won't even miss a trinket or two."

And that was what was bothering me. Any thief worth his salt should have taken a lot more. I decided not to bother explaining this to Harlow. Time to change the subject. "I'm guessing NEC&I is not the only company you do business with."

He gave me a smug grin. "Of course not. I use a specialty company for my truly high-value clients. You folks are for my run-of-the-mill business, you know, walk-ins and the like."

I forced myself to ignore the obvious insult. "Which company is that?" I asked. *McMansions Are Us, perhaps?*

"I'd rather not say."

That was not a surprise. I glanced over at the empty desk. "Do you have any other employees?"

"No. Just Irina. With upload and download and everything being computerized, I only need one girl."

I bristled at his use of the word "girl", then forced myself to ignore his obvious chauvinism for the time being. In case he had something important to say.

"And this one is a lot better than the last girl," he continued. "Far more reliable. The last one simply disappeared one day. Just up and vanished. Didn't show up for work. Didn't call. I never heard from her again."

That was disturbing. "And you weren't able to locate her? You must have had her phone number. And her address."

Harlow shrugged. "I meant to call. Then, somehow, I never got to it. Life got busy. I had to move on."

"What was her name?" I asked.

"That's none of your business. So if there's nothing else ... "

"I'd like to take a look at those files now please."

"Files? Are you living in the Dark Ages? People don't use paper files anymore. Everything's computerized these days."

"Then I'd like to look at your computer files," I said, struggling to control my growing anger.

"That's not going to happen. Sorry. Too much privileged information in them. I can't go putting it on display for just anybody." He looked at his watch. "And I will need to be going in a few minutes. Sorry."

Son of a bitch! This was not at all acceptable. And I wasn't "just anybody." I took a deep breath to keep myself from saying anything rude. I decided not to fight with the man today. I'd find another way to get the information I needed. Then I'd be back with a vengeance. "I guess that's all for now Mr. Harlow" I said. "We'll be back in touch." *And, just for the record, plenty of offices out there still use paper files. And there's nothing wrong with that!*

His look said "Whatever."

Count on it. I didn't like the man. I walked back to my Mustang more determined than ever to get to the bottom of these jewel thefts, with or without his help.

I was officially discouraged. I'd visited three offices and, one way or another, been blown off by all of them. I could understand Jose Almeida's issues, but Tom Foye's made no sense at all. And Harlow was a rude SOB. Not only that, but the women who worked for both Foye and Harlow showed little respect for their bosses. Was this what it was like working in a small business these days? I certainly hoped not. The question of the moment was: what did these three agencies have in common that would make them, or their clients, targets for a jewel thief? There had to be something there. Something I was missing.

Chapter 9

I popped into the coffee shop near where I'd parked and got a chicken salad sandwich and a bottle of water to go. I scarfed the sandwich down in the car, took a big swig of water, then dialed Peggy before pulling out. I can talk and drive just fine. Eating and driving is another story.

"Excuse me for mentioning this, but didn't we just speak a little while ago?" she teased.

"That's true. But I'm frustrated and need to vent. Please tell me you and Tiffany have found something of interest. I need some good news right now. The agent in Cotuit left me in a nasty mood."

"While we are in hot pursuit of the facts," she replied, "there is nothing of interest to report yet. Sorry."

"You're forgiven."

"Thanks," she said. "I guess we're all having a bad day. Or at least an unproductive one. Other than the questions we discussed earlier, have you seen any unusual commonality with the agents you've visited?"

I gave that some thought. "There are interesting dynamics in all three offices, that's for sure. Two of the three owners don't have much of a handle on what's going on. It's understandable with Jose Almeida. He's grieving for his late son. And Lord knows what's up with Tom Foye. I guess I'll have to wait until I hear from him again to know more about that. But in both cases, this lack of control could lead to trouble for NEC&I."

"Do you think their claim results slipped due to poor management?" Peggy asked. "Or is there something more nefarious going on?"

"Anything is possible at this point. The third owner, Francis Harlow, appears to be on top of things just fine, but he's a rude SOB and not at all interested in working with us."

"What about the office staff?"

"Nothing jumps out at me. Two are young. Two are middle-aged. At least two appear to have little respect for their boss. And one of them has apparently vanished into thin air."

"Say that again, please."

"Harlow told me she simply disappeared. And that is the next assignment for Tiffany, if you'd be good enough to pass it on. Have her do some research on the Harlow Agency in Cotuit. They had an employee who left about a year ago. The underwriter should remember her. Have Tiffany get a name then see what she can find out about her. According to the owner, she simply failed to show up one day. I'd like to learn what happened to her."

"Will do. I'll add it to our other current research projects. You know how much Tiff and I both love a good mystery."

And I was glad they did.

"Let's not lose hope yet," I said. "Something's bound to hit one of us eventually."

"Will we see your smiling face today?" she asked.

"Sorry. No can do. I'm heading back to Massapoag Junction. Sam is there helping Pete get settled into his new house. I'll do my bit as well. Sam and I probably won't get back to Cambridge until sometime this evening."

"What about tomorrow? Will we see you then?" she asked.

"I'm afraid not. Remember, I'll be visiting agents in Oxford and Sterling."

There was a moment of silence. I could hear the wheels turning in Peggy's head. "Oh, right. I did know that. Just forgot it for a moment. So now you know I'm not perfect."

I laughed. "Don't worry. I won't spread it around."

"Thanks. Now tell me, since you're heading west tomorrow, wouldn't it make more sense to spend the night at Pete's?" she asked. "It'd make for a shorter drive in the morning."

She wasn't wrong about that. "True." I said, "But Sam and I still live in Cambridge, and will continue to do so for the foreseeable future. I don't want to set a precedent this soon after Pete's move. Besides, I don't have a change of business clothes with me."

"I see what you mean."

"I'll be by the office early tomorrow morning. To drop off some files and pick up what I'll need for the next few days."

"Or, as I previously suggested, you could simply use your laptop. It has all the information you need."

"Maybe," I said. "Maybe not. And electronic devices sometimes malfunction. I'd feel better having the paper files as back-up. Anyway, I doubt if I'll see you in the morning. I want to get an early start."

She asked, "Would you like me to pop in on Sam tomorrow? I haven't seen him in a while and it's supposed to be a nice day. I bet he'd love a walk."

Peggy and Sam were good friends, and I liked for him to get out during the day whenever possible. "That would be wonderful. Thanks. I owe you one."

"And one more thing," Peggy said.

"What's that?"

"Don't forget to charge your laptop."

"Right." I laughed, I ended the call and hit the gas hard as I pulled onto Route 6 West. Despite its age, my Mustang responded with its usual enthusiasm. I did love that car.

A little over an hour later, I was in Massapoag Junction. I pulled into Pete's new driveway to find him and Sam playing Frisbee in the front yard—despite the gloomy drizzle.

"Hi, guys. It's good to see you working hard," I said.

Pete laughed. "Just taking a little break. We've been at it all day, you know, unpacking boxes, arranging furniture. We're making wonderful progress. The only thing I have yet to unpack is the kitchen. So I guess that means you and I will be dining out again."

"Or we could order some pizza. Check out that place on Main Street. We could eat it here while we work on the kitchen. That way, I won't be too late getting back to Cambridge."

"Good idea," Pete said as his smile faded.

I breathed a sigh of relief, pleased he had the good sense not to push me to stay another night. We needed to set limits somewhere. Needed to take our time. I loved Pete, but his move to a land beyond the suburbs was a big change for both of us, and I didn't want to jump into anything too quickly. We'd sort it all out in time.

I opened a bottle of Pinot Noir while Pete called for pizza. We toasted his new home then chatted as we unpacked and stowed dishes, glasses and pots and pans.

"My new homeowners policy arrived in today's mail," he told me. "I can't believe how fast that was."

"Technology is a wonderful thing." I almost surprised myself by admitting that.

"I was hoping you'd take a look at it for me, to make sure I got it right. Also, there's a questionnaire enclosed. I may need your help with that."

I was a little disappointed he hadn't put his new homeowners insurance with NEC&I, but it had been important to him to do business locally. And the only agent in town didn't represent us. I understood. The policy looked fine. The questionnaire was standard issue. Nothing to be concerned about.

"I'm thinking perhaps I should add that Special Computer Coverage," Pete said. "I paid a lot for my new desktop and printer."

"Good idea."

He paused, then added, "And I'm not sure what to do about scheduled jewelry coverage. I'm thinking I may need it."

That got my attention. "Other than your watch, which, by the way, is a thing of beauty, I didn't realize you had any expensive jewelry"

"Just one item," he said, avoiding eye contact. "My mother's engagement ring. She gave it to me a couple of months ago. She'd developed bad arthritis in her hands and couldn't get the ring over her knuckles. She thought I would want it someday, so why not give it to me now.

Oh dear! "Why don't you just keep it in a safety deposit box at the bank?"

He stumbled for a moment, then said, "I think I'd rather have it here with me. But I will get it scheduled on my policy, just as soon as I locate the appraisal. Or perhaps get a new one. To be sure of the value."

The pizza delivery guy arrived at that very moment, so I didn't have to continue that conversation. As soon as we sat down to eat, I changed the subject. "Did you meet any more of your neighbors today?"

He shook his head. "Nope. But I did have another conversation with Martha Randall. The woman is a wonderful source of random information."

"Such as?"

Pete thought for a moment. "Laura Mankin across the street is having an affair."

I groaned. "Does that make you worry at all about what she may begin telling people about us?"

"Not at all." He gave me a phony leer.

"Did Martha have any other tidbits?"

Pete thought for a moment. "As a matter of fact, yes she did. She told me to stay away from Mountain Road at all costs."

"Where's Mountain Road?"

"Not far from here. Between Bay Road in Easton and East Street in Sharon, sort of next to Massapoag Junction. From what she tells me, the road is haunted."

"Good thing to know. Did she mention what makes her believe that?"

"Not exactly, though she did say it's a dead zone," Pete said.

"A what?" I asked.

"A dead zone. You know, a place where your cell phone won't work. And neither will your car radio or your GPS."

The woman sounded like a real piece of work. "I will bear that in mind when I'm driving in the area." I sat back and thought for a minute. "I've got to tell you, Pete, I'm a little concerned about you in this town. First that woman was mugged—and killed. Now there's a dead zone up the street. Massapoag Junction is one strange place. Not to mention that slightly odd Irish restaurant in Sharon."

"I'm sure it's all fine," he said, "but what about you? How did your meetings go today? Did you make any headway?"

I shook my head. "Nothing substantial yet. The agent in Falmouth was a lost soul trying to deal with the death of his son. I don't think he's all that interested in what happens in his agency anymore. The fellow in Cotuit was a pompous ass. He blew me off and looked down his nose at me while doing it."

"What about the guy in Fall River?" he asked.

"That's a good question." I proceeded to fill him in on both the visit and the phone message. "I don't know what to make of it. I don't know whether I'm intrigued or pissed off."

Pete furrowed his brow for a moment, as if in deep thought. "Maybe try being hopeful. Perhaps whatever he has to tell you will provide the key to solving your entire investigation."

"Right. Either that or he's just some sad old guy looking for a little attention."

"Another possibility, to be sure. But don't give up on him until you hear what he has to say. You might be surprised what some sad old guy may have up his sleeve."

"You mean like maybe he'll solve my whole case before I even get started?"

"You never know," Pete said.

"As nice as that sounds," I replied, "I doubt that will be the case. There's something bigger going on here. Bigger than any of the three people I interviewed today. Something that's happening across the whole state. I need to do better tomorrow. If we don't get this thing figured out soon, as Mark so aptly put it, NEC&I could end up bleeding diamonds."

Chapter 10

I made a quick trip into the office at the crack of dawn on Tuesday, long before anybody else was around and about. Peggy had left the files I needed on my desk. I grabbed them, penned her a quick note, then dashed back to my apartment to study the files while I enjoyed my coffee. Might as well arrive prepared at today's appointments. I even spent some time with the computer files, just to be thorough. And to make Peggy proud of me.

Awake and informed, I hit the road a little before 8:30. My first destination, the town of Oxford, was allegedly an hour west on the Massachusetts Turnpike, aka Route 90. Even heading in the opposite direction of the morning commute, the trip still took me an hour and a half. That was fine. I didn't need to be there until 10:30.

The signage as I entered Oxford informed me that the town was first settled in the late 1600s, had a population of nearly 14,000 and was the birthplace of Clara Barton, founder of the American Red Cross. Who knew? The nearest large city was Worcester.

My destination, the Zoltov Agency, was in an old building in an older part of town. It looked tired, and perhaps a little sad. I pulled up in front, took one last look at the file and locked my Mustang before heading in. According to what I had read, the owner of the Zoltov Agency was named Charlie Fitzmaurice. Funny, I would have expected someone of Russian background. Silly me.

The agency had been with NEC&I for a dozen years, with relatively few issues until a few years ago. There had been a recent change in ownership. Maybe that could explain the current performance problems.

Fitzmaurice met me at the door. He was middle-aged, short and paunchy, but looking very business-like in a dark blue suit, white shirt and pin-striped tie. "Good morning, Ms. Lynch."

I shook his hand. "It's good to meet you."

"And this here is Maureen," he said, indicating a woman seated at a desk nearby. "My right-hand man, so to speak."

Maureen was thirty-something and almost pretty, with jet black hair and green eyes nearly as nice as Pete's. She smiled up at me from a mass of paperwork on her desk. "Nice to meet you, Ms. Lynch. Oops. I'm afraid you'll have to excuse me." She turned to answer her ringing phone.

"Please come into my office and sit down," Fitzmaurice said. "And we can have a nice long talk. But first, can I get you some coffee? Or tea perhaps?"

"No thank you. I'm fine." I followed him to his office, seated myself and pulled out his file.

The man looked everywhere except in my direction. "I understand you're concerned about some losses we've had lately?" he said.

"That's correct."

"I've been worried sick about this ever since I got the call from you folks." He stared down at his shaking hands. "I spent hours last night poring over the files you mentioned. They all look to me like fairly ordinary theft losses."

"True enough. The issue is more that there are so many of them." I sat back to let that sink in with him.

Fitzmaurice's shoulders slumped ever so slightly. "I'm new to the insurance business, you see. I only bought this place a year ago. Got it for a song when the former owner retired. I'm still learning the ropes, so to speak. Trying hard to make a go of it, and hoping I haven't made a mistake." He stared down at a pile of papers on his desk, as if perhaps they contained the answer.

Against my better judgment, my heart went out to the guy.

"I'm getting the hang of how insurance works," he continued. "And I've got to tell you, it's a lot more complicated than I would have thought." He shook his head. "Maureen has been a wonderful help. She was here with the prior owner, and was happy to stay on with me."

"Is she your only employee?" I asked.

"At the moment, yes. There was another woman. She chose to move on when I purchased the business. I need to find someone else soon. This office is too busy for just myself and Maureen."

"It's a good thing Maureen didn't decide to leave when the other woman did," I said.

"It is indeed. Truth be told, I don't know what I'd do without her. She's so good with the clients. Good to them as well. Always seeing to their needs. Asking if they've made any recent purchases, bought something that may need special coverage. Have they started a business in their home? She asks everybody. Always. Don't get me wrong. She doesn't try to sell them anything they don't need. But always makes sure they have what they do need." He paused to come up for air.

I sat and waited.

"Maureen even sells a few Personal Umbrella policies, if you can believe that," he added. "As if anybody out here is likely to get sued for millions of dollars."

Interesting, but not quite unbelievable.

"So what's the problem with my losses?" he asked.

"Jewelry thefts, to be specific."

He nodded. "Right. There have been a few of those lately. I was surprised to learn we insure as much jewelry as we do. I didn't expect it in such a small town. We don't even have a local jewelry store. Folks have to go all the way into Worcester to buy nice jewelry or to get an appraisal. But I'm still not sure I see the problem. I figured that's what this business is all about. Taking care of people when they have a loss. Am I missing something?"

"There have been a lot of jewelry thefts state-wide this past year," I told him. "Much more than you would normally expect. And always high-valued items, mostly diamonds. We're trying to get a handle on what's happening before it gets any worse."

"Oh dear. That is a worry. Exactly how much trouble am I in? I can't afford to lose my contract with you. NEC&I is my only company at the moment. I know I need to have more than one, but that's not easy when I don't have much of a track record."

"You're not in trouble with us," I told him. *At least not yet.* "This problem goes far beyond your agency."

A look of relief washed over his face.

"We're hoping you can work with us to put an end to these thefts," I continued. "Right about now, we'll take all the assistance we can get."

"How could I be of help to you?"

"By providing us with as much information as possible on these losses. We need to find a common thread between your theft losses and others that we've experienced across the state in the past year."

He shook his head. "That sounds like an ambitious undertaking, to be sure. But I'll do my level best."

"I'd like to take a look at your files now, please."

"Not a problem. Got them right here." He indicated a large pile of files on his desk.

"We'd also like you to discuss the losses with Maureen. Please review your files with her and look for anything those clients may have in common. Do they all live in the same neighborhood? Are these people related to each other in any way?"

"Or go to the same church?" Fitzmaurice said. "I think I'm beginning to see what you're after. Anything that might connect them to each other."

"That's right. Or connect each of them to the burglar. Or are there any similarities in the ways their thefts occurred?"

"That's a tall order, Ms. Lynch, but I'll set myself to it right away."

"We'd appreciate that. And please keep Maureen involved. I'm sure she's known your clients a lot longer than you have. She may see, or know, something that you don't about them."

Fitzmaurice nodded. "Excellent idea. I will do exactly that."

I spent the next hour or so examining the files. They were neat and well-kept, and loaded with documentation of all sorts, as well as a lot of personal correspondence and notes from meetings with clients. The only problem was, there was not one scrap of information helpful to my investigation. I began to wonder why I even bothered looking in agents' files. I'd probably never discover a smoking gun in any of them.

While I read the files, I eavesdropped on Maureen as she spoke on the phone with customers or helped a few who came into the office. She was wonderful with people. I did, however, give up on the idea of interviewing her. It was obvious to me that the office was far too busy for that at the moment. I'd figure out how to deal with that later. I also listened in on a few of Fitzmaurice's phone conversations and decided that the man was overly modest. He sounded both professional and knowledgeable. The Zoltov Agency was a well-run operation. So, in light of all that, what was up with the increase in their losses?

Closing the final file, I said to Fitzmaurice, "Thank you for your time. I'll be back in touch. Or call me with anything you may discover." And I believed he would. It was nice to find an agent willing—and apparently able—to work with me. I hoped this would morph into a trend. Fast.

I said good-bye to a much-relieved Charlie Fitzmaurice and walked up the street to the diner on the corner. I had just about enough time to eat something before driving to Sterling for my next appointment. It was important. I didn't think so well on an empty stomach.

While drinking my tea and waiting for my BLT, I checked my email. Most of it could wait. A note from Peggy worried me, though. She said that George was getting all bent out of shape with the amount of time Tiffany was spending on the jewelry theft project. He was afraid she was neglecting her other work. That made little sense to me. After all, this was only day two of Tiffany's current assignment, not to mention that this entire investigation began with George bringing the diamond theft issue to our attention. Perhaps George simply felt the need for something to crank about.

I emailed back to see if George had discussed his concerns with Tiffany. Peggy's response: "Of course not." Some things never changed.

There was also an email from George informing me of another large jewelry loss. He never mentioned anything about Tiffany. Nor did he provide any useful details about this newest loss. I responded to him, asking for specifics—as in any and all information he had—and asking him to share it with Peggy and Tiffany as well. I bcc'd Peggy on this so it wouldn't slip through any unknown cracks. Another theft loss was not good news. NEC&I had sprung a leak. We needed to plug it before our corporate vessel sank.

Chapter 11

En route to the Maxwell Agency in Sterling, I reviewed my conversation with Charlie Fitzmaurice. One thing he had said that piqued my interest was that his clients had to go to Worcester for their jewelry appraisals. That got me thinking about jewelry appraisals in general. Where in Worcester did they go? Did they all use the same jeweler? Might this be the commonality we were hoping to find? The leak that was funneling information to the jewel thief, or thieves? The idea was at least worth looking into. I pulled off the road and into a CVS parking lot, then texted Peggy to add this thought to her already-massive load of research to be done. Our underwriting files should contain copies of jewelry appraisals. Maybe it wasn't much of a lead, but it was a place to start.

I arrived in Sterling in no time. The sign which welcomed me also announced that the town dated back to 1720, had a population under 8,000 and was the home of the Wachusett Mountain Ski Area. It was a charming little place if you're big into small town living. Fine for a long weekend. Otherwise not quite my style.

I spent a few minutes re-reading the paper file on the Maxwell Agency. The computer version would have to wait because I had forgotten to charge my laptop. I knew it was theoretically possible to access this from my phone, but was hopelessly inept at doing so, despite the many times Peggy had shown me. The paper file worked just fine for me. From what I saw, the agency was average in every way. They were profitable enough and had stayed off our radar for the last forty years—until recently. Their underwriter loved them. I hoped I would as well.

The office was located in a strip mall on the western end of Main Street, so I passed by pretty much everything the town had to offer. I wondered what the residents did once the sun went down.

A tall, willowy brunette wearing jeans torn at the knee and high-heeled boots was seated at a desk doodling on a file folder. She turned the folder over, then greeted me with enthusiasm. "Hello. You must be Amy from the insurance company. I'm Kate. It's so nice to see you. I've been looking forward to meeting you. We don't get many visitors out here in the sticks. Other than the local clients, that is."

She had known I was coming, yet she hadn't bothered to dress for the occasion. What was up with that? "Pleased to meet you." I struggled to match her enthusiasm, but fell sadly short.

"Mr. Maxwell's in his office," she continued. "I'll let him know you're here." She popped into the other room and was back in a flash. "Sorry. He's on the phone. Why don't you have a seat? Can I get you some coffee?"

"No thanks. Do you have any idea how long he'll be?"

Kate shrugged. "That's a very good question. He tends to spend a lot of time on the phone. Works very hard to do his best for the clients. I've got to give him credit for that. The man puts his whole heart and soul into the job. It breaks my heart to see him having such a streak of bad luck."

I wasn't sure how to respond to that. Instead of trying, I asked "Is this a busy office?"

She shook her head. "Not as a rule. A busy day might consist of a handful of phone calls and one or two clients coming in, if we're lucky. It gets a little lonely."

"I'm sorry to hear that," I said. "What do you do to pass the time?"

"I do everything I can to think up ways to grow this business, attract new customers, upsell to existing ones. Anything to make a success of things."

"I hope Mr. Maxwell pays you well for your efforts."

"That'd be nice," she said. "A good-sized raise in pay might make living in this one-horse town worth my while. It's boring as all get-out. There's nowhere to go, nothing to do and nobody to do it with."

I couldn't help but ask, "Then why do you stay?"

"My mom needs me. She isn't doing so well since my dad died last year. I moved in with her a few months ago. I needed to keep an eye on her, make sure she's all right. Now she refuses to abandon her home of forty years to move somewhere else with me. So I simply can't leave. I'm all she's got. Besides, I'm fond of Earl. He's been good to me. I don't want to move away and leave him high and dry."

"He's lucky to have you," I told her.

Kate sighed. "I've got to tell you, though, I sure do miss Brenda."

"Who is that?"

"Brenda used to work here. Part-time. We were both part-time with two hours of overlap in the middle of the day. She and I were friends. I was sorry when she left."

"How long ago did she leave?"

"A couple of months."

"Do you know why she left?"

Kate furrowed her brow. "I'm not sure. Something happened between her and Earl. I don't know what. Brenda didn't want to talk about it. And from the day she left, Earl has never even mentioned her name."

Now that caught my attention. "It looks like he's off the phone now," I said as a tall, rangy man with a bushy blonde mustache emerged from the other room.

Kate jumped to attention. "What's up, Earl? Anything I need to know about?" she asked.

He shrugged. "Nothing much, I'm sorry to say." He looked at me. "Are you my 2:00 appointment?" he asked.

I handed him my card. "Yes. Amy Lynch, from NEC&I," I said. "It's nice to meet you."

"Right. You too. How about we talk in my office?" He smiled at Kate as he said this. "You're in charge out here. Call me if you need anything."

She nodded and returned to her desk.

"Come right this way, please." Maxwell ushered me into his tiny but tidy office. He took a deep breath, then let it out slowly.

The poor man looked like he was on the verge of a stroke.

I began with the easy stuff. "As I understand it, the Maxwell Agency is part of a larger enterprise, with five separate offices located in the greater Worcester area, each with a different name, but common owners."

"That's right," he answered, but didn't offer any additional information.

"Why not use a single name for the group?" I asked.

"I wondered about that as well. Apparently, the owners want folks to feel that they're doing business with somebody small and local. They feel it's friendlier that way. Makes people feel at home."

He may have been right about that.

"So you're an employee of the agency, not a principal owner?" I asked.

He frowned. "I'm just an employee."

I wondered if that might somehow make a difference. "Of the five Maxwell offices, where does yours fit in with regard to size?"

"We're the smallest."

Oh dear. That was a problem. I had reviewed the loss results for all five locations. This one's record was by far the worst.

Maxwell fidgeted in his chair. "So, I ... uh ... understand you want to talk about something specific?"

"That's right. We're interested in the jewelry thefts your agency has had in the past several months. My assistant should have given you the names on those losses when she called. I was hoping you'd have a chance to review the files before I got here."

"I looked them over this morning. I just don't know what to tell you, though. What exactly are you looking for?"

"You've had a number of large thefts," I said. "Burglaries. Expensive jewelry items taken. Mostly diamonds." I pulled his file from my briefcase and showed him his loss record for the last twelve months. "Of the five locations, yours has had the largest number of burglaries."

He hung his head. "Yeah. I know. We've had a bad year. Things were going so well for us a while back. Then it all just went straight to Hell. I know things don't look too good for us. We've had the same problems with our other company, and now they're threatening to cancel our contract. Please tell me you're not here to cut us off as well. Or to convince the owners to shut down this location. I need my job. And Kate needs hers as well."

I forced a smile. "We're not here to cancel your contract or close you down, Mr. Maxwell. We're just trying to get our heads around this rash of jewelry thefts. And it's not just from you. It's from several other agencies as well."

That fact seemed to comfort him. "Do you think there's a big-time jewel thief on the loose in Massachusetts?"

"Something like that," I said. "We're hoping you can help us figure it out." I sat back to collect my thoughts, then tried a different tack. "I must admit I was surprised to learn that a small town agency of your size writes so much scheduled jewelry coverage."

Maxwell nodded. "To tell you the truth, so was I. But Kate's good at selling it. She says that most married women have at least one piece of good jewelry, a diamond engagement ring. And that they're happy to buy coverage to protect it. It seems that she's right."

Apparently so. But how did it fit into my case?

I stayed for a while looking through their files. Once again, nothing notable.

I left Sterling on the verge of being discouraged once more. The people I'd spoken with today were nice enough, and they all were trying to be helpful. But I felt like I was getting nowhere. I'd visited five agents so far and was no closer to solving the puzzle than I was on Monday. I gritted my teeth. The answer was out there somewhere. And I intended to find it, one way or another. I'd need to go back to my office one day soon, and I didn't want to walk in empty-handed.

Chapter 12

I chatted with Peggy on speaker phone as I drove home on the Mass Pike. The initial reason for the call was to ask her to pull the files for my agency visits on Thursday as well as to check on any progress she and Tiffany were making with their end of the investigation.

"We began with your top priority," she said. "The Foye Agency in Fall River. Sally French is their underwriter. Both she and her assistant Lily were happy to fill me in on the goings-on there."

"Goings on?" I asked, ever hopeful.

"Nothing note-worthy, I'm sorry to say. But curious nevertheless. They don't know Tom very well. He hasn't been there all that long. And they usually deal with Patti anyway. They've known her for ages. For the record, her full name is Patricia Maguire Foye."

That got my attention. "Foye?"

"Right. She's Tom Foye's sister-in-law. Was married to his late brother Nathan. Did he not mention that to you?"

"No, he didn't. And that strikes me as rather odd."

"Exactly," Peggy said. "And believe it or not, she's also his land-lady. He lives on the first floor of her two-family house in Fall River."

"You're kidding!"

"Nope. Even I couldn't make this stuff up. Sally says Patti's awful to Tom. Treats him badly. Rules his life."

From what I had seen, that came as no surprise. "You've got to wonder why he puts up with it," I said.

"Sally had the scoop on that. Apparently the Underwriting Department is one big rumor mill. From what Sally was told by the prior underwriter, Tom is beholden to Patti because of some old business venture with his brother, her late husband, which went bust and left them all nearly bankrupt. And Patti is devoting the rest of her life to making Tom pay for it."

"This is beginning to sound like a rather bad soap opera."

Peggy laughed. "I'm with you on that. It seems Patti seldom lets Tom out of her sight, except on weekends."

"What's up with weekends?" I asked.

"Apparently Tom spends them on Block Island. He goes there by himself. Every weekend. All year long. Nobody seems to know how he manages to get away from Patti like that. Or why she doesn't stop him."

I mulled that over. "I wonder if she actually could stop him."

"Or why she would want to," Peggy said. "Rumor is that he has a gay lover there, but there's no real proof to back it up."

"And no good reason why anybody would care," I said. "It seems like truth certainly is stranger than fiction, at least in this case. Now it's got me wondering if Tom has something to tell me that he doesn't want Patti to overhear. That might explain his cryptic phone message."

"My thought exactly," Peggy said.

"Anything else of interest at the moment?"

"Nothing major. I got your text about the appraisals. Tiffany and I are working on it. Nothing to report so far," she informed me, "but not to worry. We are busily pursuing all avenues of inquiry as requested by you. And we will leave no stone unturned."

"There is one additional stone I'd like Tiffany to turn."

"What's that?"

"The Maxwell Agency in Sterling had a CSR named Brenda. She left a few months ago. It's not clear exactly why. Have Tiff see what she can find out about her. And why she left."

"Will do. And then, before you know it, Tiffany and I will come up with a break-through both startling and brilliant which will allow you to solve the case and amaze the powers that be."

Peggy was nothing if not optimistic. She also made me laugh. That was the true reason for my call, whether I realized it or not. "Let's hope it all works out that way. And soon. I have to tell you, I'm more than a little disheartened with the way this case is going at the moment. I've visited five different agencies in the past few days and feel like I've learned absolutely nothing of value."

"I would guess you actually have learned something," she said. "You just don't realize it yet. You haven't had the chance to put it all together. We've only been at this for two days. I bet you an afternoon off that one of us will have this all figured out by the middle of next week."

"With an attitude like that, how could we not? I'm feeling better already. And I hope you win the bet. You deserve some time off, maybe even an entire day."

"Glad I could oblige."

"I'll be stopping at the office on my way home. Will you still be there?"

"Probably not," she said. "I have to dash out of here shortly for a dentist appointment."

"Another one? What's up with your teeth?"

"Proper dental care is important."

"True enough. And thanks for helping with Sam today. I'll talk to you tomorrow."

When I arrived home, Sam greeted me with a wagging tail and his version of a grin the minute I walked into my apartment. It's nice to be missed. We had a quick walk, then I fed him and ate an early dinner by myself. Leftovers and a large glass of my favorite Sauvignon Blanc. I filled Sam in on the events of the day. He didn't have much to offer about his own day, but, as always, he listened with rapt attention. I looked over the underwriting and claim files for my appointment the next day. Around 8:30, Sam and I went out for our evening constitutional. It was as good for me as it was for him. A healthy dose of night air always helped us both to sleep better.

We walked a couple of blocks in comfortable silence. I began to unwind. It was a pleasant evening. Mild weather always brought my neighbors out of their respective lairs. I didn't know most of their names, but recognized many of them just the same. There was the woman who walked her cat on a leash. I saw her a lot. She was nicely off-beat. Also the guy with the blue VW bug, the old guy with the long gray beard and the woman with the walker.

We greeted each other as usual, passed a few moments together, then moved on. East Cambridge was a friendly neighborhood. A nice place to live.

As we turned the corner onto Third Street, Sam spotted somebody new. I'd never seen the fellow before either, but was always happy to meet a neighbor. Also always on my guard. I had encountered the occasional creep in the past. Seldom a good experience. Nevertheless, I started out with a positive attitude.

"Good evening," I said to him as I fingered the pepper spray in my pocket.

"Hello. Nice night, isn't it?" he said.

So far so good.

He moved closer to me, uncomfortably so. Close enough for me to note his obvious lack of proper dental hygiene—Peggy would be appalled—and the droop in his left eyelid. Could he even see out of that eye?

"That's a nice dog you've got there. A really nice dog," he said.

"He sure is." I forced a smile.

"What's his name?"

"Sam."

"It's nice to meet you, Sam," he said.

Sam wagged his tail. He always knew when he was being discussed. And he loved it.

The stranger's lips morphed into something between a crooked smile and a sneer. He reached down and scratched Sam behind the ears. Sam sniffed and took a few steps back. The hair on his spine stood up, as if in the canine equivalent of goosebumps. That put me on yellow alert.

"I bet he's wonderful protection for you," the stranger said. "Protection can be so important in a city neighborhood, don't you think?"

"Absolutely." *And don't you dare forget it, Buster.* I was beginning to feel more than a little uncomfortable. Also grateful I'd remembered my pepper spray.

"Are you good at protecting him as well?"

That did it! I needed to get away from this creep. On full red alert now, I scanned both sides of the street and spotted a woman who lived next door to me. Luckily, I knew her name. "Allie," I called to her. "Wait up a sec. I have something to ask you."

Allie stopped and waited for me to join her. Sam and I crossed the street. My creepy friend slithered away and the world was right again. At least for the moment.

I had a brief conversation with Allie, said good night and dashed into my building, making certain the front door was locked behind me. I held my breath until Sam and I reached my third floor apartment and bolted the door. Then I called Pete.

I told him what had happened and was feeling pretty pleased about the way I had handled the encounter.

Pete wasn't so pleased. "Did you call the police?"

"No."

"And why not?"

"I wasn't sure what I'd tell them."

"How about that somebody threatened you?"

"At least I thought he did. And that's the problem. Perhaps I simply misinterpreted what he said."

"Or not. This type of thing has happened to you more than once before. I worry about you living alone in the city, Ames. It can be a dangerous place."

"I'm not exactly alone, you know. Sam would make mincemeat out of anybody who tried to do me harm."

"That's true. Nevertheless ... "

"Nevertheless nothing, Pete. And if I'm not mistaken, wasn't there a woman mugged and murdered in Massapoag Junction recently as well? So how much safer is it there?"

He had no answer for that.

I chose not to gloat.

"Did the incident shake you up?" he asked. "Do you want me to come over and keep you safe and warm?"

"That's not necessary. I'm fine."

I could almost hear Pete rolling his eyes. "Fine for now, sure. Please, promise me that next time something like this happens you will call the police."

"If you insist. In the meantime, I'm tired. I had a busy day today. And I'll be on the road again tomorrow. I'm driving out to Lee, so it'll be a long day. I just wanted to hear your voice and tell you I love you before I called it a night."

We both knew that I was lying. Not the part about loving him. That was true. I was lying about being fine. That was all right, though. I would be eventually.

For the moment, though, I had a case to investigate. A puzzle to solve. And a good night's sleep would help me do that. In the immortal words of Scarlett O'Hara, "Tomorrow is another day." I hoped it would be a good one.

Chapter 13

I spent an hour or so the next morning reviewing the paper files for the agent I was meeting today, hoping to spot anything I may have previously missed. I tried not to let my lack of progress get me down. It wasn't easy. I also scanned the computerized files. Peggy would be proud of me. I learned that for the last forty years, the Berkshire Insurance Agency had been one of our best-performing agents. Their losses were low, their production high and their problems few and far between. Until recently, that is, when our mysterious jewel thieves hit them with a vengeance. I needed to learn why, and how.

My plan was to leave late enough to miss the morning traffic. Our appointment was set for 1:00. It was a long ride to Lee, all the way to the opposite end of the state. At least two hours driving, and that was not including pit stops. I'd spent a lot of time on the Massachusetts Turnpike lately. It was a boring road. I decided to bring Sam with me. I could use the company, and I never felt quite right talking to myself, even in the car. Talking to Sam helped me stay alert.

The town of Lee was in the middle of the Berkshire resort area—a very busy place in the summer and autumn, not so much in the early spring. It had under 6,000 inhabitants, a few nature trails, some premium outlet stores and a downtown which was on the National Register of Historic Places. I always enjoyed spending time there, though preferably when not working.

I located the Berkshire Insurance Agency with no trouble at all and managed to find a parking spot right out front. I lowered a window so Sam would have enough air, locked my Mustang and walked in.

The office was abuzz with activity. Two middle-aged women sat at their desks speaking on the phone while staring at computer screens and entering notes. A hugely pregnant red-head sat at another desk opening mail. A younger woman with long braids and a seriously-sturdy build stood at the counter helping a customer fill out some paperwork.

A twenty-something woman handed a stack of paper files to a younger girl, then approached me at the counter. She had impossibly blonde hair, too much eye liner and an odd-looking collection of green scratches on her upper arm. An infection? A tattoo gone bad, perhaps? Or was it a scar? I wished I had a band aid to give the girl.

"Help you?" she asked, snapping her gum.

"I'm Amy Lynch from New England Casualty and Indemnity," I told her. "Here to see Ernie Graham. I have an appointment."

"Right. He's expecting you," she said. "He told us to bring you straight into his office the moment you arrived. The trouble is he's on the phone right now. Do you mind waiting?'

I agreed, despite the mixed messages I was getting. I spotted a textbook on the counter for the Massachusetts Insurance Broker's licensing exam. "Studying hard?" I asked her.

She scowled. "Unfortunately so. I gotta tell you, I hate insurance."

Then why are you here? Before I had a chance to voice my question, a man approached from the rear of the office. He was sporting a well-cut three-piece blue suit, complete with white shirt and pale lavender tie, good look, but perhaps a bit much for a small town in the Berkshires. His hair looked recently styled, his tan sprayed on. I said a quick prayer he wouldn't be quite as imperious and over-the-top as he appeared and forced a smile onto my face.

"Ms. Lynch?"

"Good morning," I said as I handed him my card.

"Come this way, please. It's quieter in there, better for having a serious talk." He looked around the room and smiled. "As you were, ladies. Carry on."

A couple of the "ladies" rolled their eyes as I followed Ernie Graham to his office.

"This is a busy place," I said as I took a seat across from his desk.

"Yes, indeed," he beamed. "It's a lively little office. It keeps us all hopping. There's always something major going on. I have to admit that I like it this way. It makes the day go so much faster."

I wondered if the "ladies" liked it that way as well.

Graham folded his hands on his desk and leaned toward me. "I have to tell you, I was more than a little disconcerted when I got the call from you folks. Our loss record has always been on the low side. I'm proud of the job we do here. We're a professional office. My people are good at their jobs. I insist on everybody getting licensed and taking continuing education courses. It's important for them to know what they're doing."

I nodded. "I noticed that the lady who helped me out front was studying for the broker's license exam."

"Deirdre, right. She's new here. I don't normally hire unlicensed people but last summer I simply had no choice."

"Why is that?" I asked, hoping against hope that the reason would have some bearing on my investigation.

"I lost one of my best, most experienced people. This office is far too busy to function with one less person. I needed help fast. I found an employment agency which specializes in insurance personnel. This fellow guarantees his people are well-trained and have the proper experience. They are all either already licensed or working on it. I don't have time to train anybody myself. Nobody here does. If Deirdre is typical of the people this agent represents, I'd use him again in a heartbeat. She's a regular dynamo."

I nodded. "What's the name of this agency?"

"Insurance Personnel, Inc.," he said. "They're on Broad Street in Boston. I have to admit it surprised me that they'd have a candidate looking for work at the other end of the state."

That surprised me as well.

He shook his head. "I don't know what to think about all these jewelry thefts. I agree with you that something is obviously amiss. I only wish I knew what."

I jumped in before he had a chance to come up for air. "It's not just this office."

"Oh?" His whole body relaxed when he heard this. "Other agents are experiencing adverse loss results as well?"

"They are. We're seeing a marked increase in jewelry thefts state-wide. Mostly diamonds."

"I'm glad to know it's not just us. And I want to help you get to the bottom of this before it gets any worse."

His words were music to my ears.

"So here's what I've done so far," he continued. "I had everybody come in an hour early today for an emergency staff meeting, even the file clerk. We discussed the issue and tossed around ideas. Nothing substantial yet, but at least I've got them all thinking about jewelry, as well as thefts. We pulled the files in question and passed them out. The plan is for everybody to review their share, looking for anything that seems a little off. Or anything these clients may have in common. Like perhaps they all used the same jeweler for appraisals, or something like that. Then they'll pass the files along to the next person. That way, they'll all review the file on every problematic theft claim within the next few days. Then we'll sit down together early next week to discuss what we've found."

I struggled to keep my jaw from dropping. This guy seemed not only sincere but also eager to work with us to help figure this mess out, not to mention efficient. And to think that when I first saw the man I expected him to be a pompous ass. Shame on me for judging people by appearances. "That sounds wonderful, Mr. Graham. We appreciate your efforts."

He smiled. "No problem. We are all in this together."

I didn't see any reason for me to hang around and review their files. Better to wait and see what, if anything, they came up with. For whatever reason, I decided I could trust Ernie Graham to come through for me. I thanked him for his time as he escorted me to the door. "Oh, one more thing," I said to him.

"What's that?"

"You said you were in a hurry to replace a customer service representative."

"That's right."

"What happened to the former one?" I asked. "Did she leave suddenly? Did she give notice?"

He shook his head. "She died unexpectedly. Her canoe overturned in Laurel Lake. A real tragedy."

"I'm sorry," I told him.

He nodded. "Thanks. We all are."

On that sad note, I returned to my car.

Sam greeted me with his usual enthusiasm. I was hungry. He needed a pit stop. We headed out of Lee.

A few miles out of town, I spotted a small roadside diner with some woods behind the parking lot. The very place for all of our needs. Sam took care of business. I got two burgers to go and an order of fries. We ate them in the car. I had more fries than Sam did, but he didn't seem to mind.

My phone dinged. A voicemail had arrived while I was getting our food. I opened my bottle of water and sat back to listen to my message.

"Ms. Lynch, hi. It's me again. Tom Foye. Like I said the other day, I have some information to share with you. You need to know what's going on. I've got to tell you about the Mullins brothers. I can't tell you over the phone, though. It might not be safe. We need to have a face-to-face conversation. I have stuff to show you, stuff to give you. We definitely have to get together. But it will have to wait until this Saturday. I can't get away before that. I'll be on Block Island over the weekend. Meet me there for lunch at Dead Eye Dick's. Noon. And don't tell anybody where you're going. Please don't let me down. This is urgent business. See you then."

Now I was intrigued. Also somewhat pissed at the way he was handling this whatever-it-was, but I'd get over it. There was a distinct possibility that I may be about to catch a break here. Suddenly, Saturday couldn't come soon enough.

Chapter 14

The next morning, Tom Foye's message weighed heavily on my mind—for a number of reasons. He'd sounded so agitated, not to mention just plain scared. What in the world could he have to tell me? And who the hell were the Mullins brothers? From what Peggy had learned, I guessed our meeting had to be on Block Island so Patti wouldn't know about it. I'd never been there, but from what I knew about the place, it was primarily a summer resort. And pretty dead the rest of the year.

Something Foye said rang a bell somewhere in my memory banks. The Mullins brothers. I was convinced I'd heard that name recently but couldn't remember where. I hated it when things nagged at my brain like that. This time it had nearly spoiled a perfectly nice evening with Pete. I stayed at his place because my appointment this morning was in Washburn Falls, just a short drive from Massapoag Junction. We had dinner at a charming little Indian restaurant in Sharon and I was distracted enough that I barely tasted the food. Pete said it was quite good. I took his word for it. The Mullins brothers, whoever they were, also kept me awake half the night. Was Foye referring to a family, or a business—or a family business? Knowing that would be a good first step. And perhaps it would let me get some decent sleep.

I was not at my best in the morning. Before leaving for my appointment, I googled "Mullins Brothers" and found nothing. I also checked the NEC&I database. There were plenty of clients named Mullins, but none with any obvious connection to the Foye Agency. Where the hell had I heard that name? I willed it away from my mind for the time being. This morning's appointment was important too. I needed to concentrate on that.

I arrived at the Christopher Nevins Insurance Agency in Washburn Falls a few minutes early for my 9:30 appointment. I used the extra time to take a look at our file on them. Nevins had been with NEC&I for years. It had been one of our top agencies at one time. Then something happened to change that. It was gradual at first, and declined slowly for a few years. There had even been talk of cancelling our contract with them. Then their loss results went from poor to dismal in the past year. They were considerably worse than the other agencies on our current frequent flyers list. Something was definitely amiss. I pasted on a happy face, forced Tom Foye and the Mullins brothers from my mind and headed toward the door.

The front room of the agency was dull and grim looking. Big old wooden desks. Swivel chairs. Metal file cabinets of an indeterminate color. Still, it was neat and orderly, and appeared to be organized. There was nobody in the front room, but I heard voices coming from the back. Angry voices. One male, one female.

"What the hell is wrong with you?" the man shouted. "You work from 9:00 to noon. Every day. Which gives you the afternoon off. Every afternoon. And yet you scheduled a dentist appointment for 10:00 this morning. Where was your head?"

"I'm sorry, Chris," the woman said. "I couldn't help it. This is an emergency. I had to take what I could get. And Teresa was fine about coming in early today. She owed me a favor. So what's the big deal?"

"The big deal is that I'm in charge here," he growled. "You ladies are supposed to run stuff like this by me."

"Right. Yeah. Next time I surely will. Promise."

I cleared my throat to announce my arrival.

"Go see who that is before you leave," he barked. "I believe we're expecting that claims investigator. I'll be at my desk."

A young woman emerged from the back room. She was blonde and tiny—what my mother would call "a little slip of a thing." She wore black slacks, a green twin sweater set and a scowl on her face. "Morning. You're Amy Lynch, right?"

"I am."

She glared toward the back office. "Sorry you had to hear all that. Not very professional of us."

"It's all right. Not to worry. I've heard worse."

"Hey, Chris! That Ms. Lynch is here. From the insurance company. You know, New England Casualty and Indemnity."

Chris stormed into the main office. He was overweight and well beyond middle-age. There was an unsightly stain on his tie. "Give me a break, Alana. You don't have to tell me where she's from. I can keep track of my own business associates, you know."

"Right. Sure," she said. "So I'll be off now. See you tomorrow." She grabbed her bag and strode out the door.

Christopher Nevins glared at Alana as she left, then turned to me and shook his head. "I don't know what's wrong with young people these days. No respect for authority. Or for their elders. They all just do as they damn please." He grabbed a paper off Alana's desk. "And will you look at this. This is how she spends her time when she thinks I'm not watching. Doodling. Just get a load of this. It looks like a chicken walked across the paper with ink on its feet." He held the paper up for me to see, but too far away for me to get a good look at it. Then before I could comment on it, or ask for a better look, he tore the paper up and tossed it into the trash.

My curiosity was piqued. Sadly, there was no good way to ask to see this paper. Rather than try, I held out my hand. "It's nice to meet you, Mr. Nevins." I was probably lying.

"Yeah, right. You too. Have a seat. I've got to stay out front here until Teresa shows up. Let's hope she's on time for a change." He plopped himself down at Alana's desk.

I sat as well and opened my file with his loss results.

"I already know what you're going to say." He shook his head. "I'm in trouble with NEC&I. My losses have sky-rocketed lately. Nothing good going on in Washburn Falls these days. The whole town is going down the tubes."

"Oh? How so?" I braced myself for potential bad news.

"It's all these damn people moving here. Foreigners. Immigrants. Refugees. Whatever. They're taking the town over and driving it right into the gutter. And the damn cops don't do anything about it. What the hell do they think we pay them for?"

I bit my tongue and listened to his tirade. There was no point arguing with an angry bigot.

He calmed himself and shook his head. "It was different before. This used to be a nice place to live. The agency was doing well. When Joanie worked here, things ran like clockwork. Clients were happy. Our losses were low. And Joanie managed all that on a part-time basis. Then she left. And things here just fell apart."

"How long ago did Joanie leave?"

He furrowed his brow. "Little over a year now. I sure do miss her."

At the risk of sounding overly nosy, which I was, I asked, "Where did she go? And why?" The why of it was particularly important to me.

"She went to a good-sized agency in Dedham. They offered her a full-time position. With benefits. Her husband died unexpectedly and she needed a full-time job. And health insurance. I wasn't about to do that. Too damn expensive. And not necessary. Folks these days expect too much from a job. They want it all handed to them."

And if they were dealing with this guy, they probably earned it handily. "So what do you have now for employees?"

"Two part-timers. Alana, who just left and Teresa, who is about to be late—again." He scowled up at the clock on the wall.

Time to change the subject. "Were you able to take a look at the losses we're looking into?"

He shook his head. "Nope. Sorry. I'll try to get to it sometime today."

Bad answer. Now I needed to stay and look through his files myself. And I wanted to get out of the place as fast as I could. I didn't like this man. He was making my already cranky mood even worse. "I'd like to take a look at them while I'm here."

"Whatever."

As I was bemoaning my fate, a tall, thin red-head swept into the office, all out of breath.

"Sorry, Chris. I over-slept. Got here as fast as I could. Did I miss much?"

"Nothing, Teresa. Not one damn thing," he growled. "Ms. Lynch here is going to take a look at those files you pulled yesterday. I'll be in my office."

As he stomped away, he turned back to me and added, "Nice meeting you."

I didn't think he meant it.

Teresa gave me a tired smile. "Sorry about that. He's been in a bad temper off and on for months now. Lord knows why. Alana and I do our best to cheer him up. Some days it works. Seems like today isn't one of them. Some days I wish he'd just go home and leave it to us. I sure wish I knew what's making him so unhappy."

I'd like to know as well. "I'll just sit over there while I look at these files. I'll do my best not to be in your way."

"Oh, don't worry about that. It's nice to have somebody to talk to when things are quiet here," she said.

"Are they often quiet?"

"They sure are." She took off her coat and sat at her desk.

She was wearing a bright pink knit dress. Odd choice for a red head. I did, however, like her jewelry. "Is that a Claddagh pin?" I asked.

"Sure is. It was my grandmother's. She left it to me in her will. I've always loved it."

"Your grandmother was Irish?" I asked.

"Indeed she was. Right off the boat from the old country."

The phone rang, Teresa answered it and I sat to check out the files. As pleasant as Teresa was, I needed to finish quickly and get to my own office. The files didn't contain anything of interest, just the usual paperwork. No obvious commonality, either to the other Nevins files or to any of the losses I'd reviewed elsewhere over the past few days. The only difference here was that more of Alana's doodles showed up every now and again. I was thinking the poor girl must be horribly bored with her job when I took a closer look at the so-called doodles. They bore a remarkable likeness to the Celtic ogham writing I had seen in Ireland. Was that just a fluke? Or could it be deliberate? I found myself wishing I'd paid more attention to the things my father had told me when we were touring the Irish countryside. I availed myself of Nevins' office machinery and photocopied the paperwork in question. I'd take a better look at it later. Sadly, that was my only take-away from my visit to the Nevins Agency. I never made it to the wastebasket to get a look at Alana's other doodles. I made a note to have a chat with their underwriter. If Nevins treated his clients as rudely as he did both me and his employees, I questioned whether or not we'd want to continue our relationship with him. His attitude could reflect badly on NEC&I. For the moment, though, I simply wanted to pack up and head to Cambridge. Maybe Peggy and Tiffany would have something useful for me. Maybe they'd know something about the mysterious Mullins brothers.

Chapter 15

I stopped by Pete's to pick up Sam, then headed back to Cambridge. The look on Sam's face suggested he'd rather be chasing squirrels in Pete's yard, or barking at the ducks. "Sorry, Buddy," I told him. "It's time to go home. I'm sure you'll be happy to be back in your own bed." I wasn't sure he believed me.

Sam and I said good-bye to Pete and set out for Cambridge.

I settled Sam at home, gave him a treat, and walked to the office. It felt good to get some fresh air and exercise after spending most of the week in my car. That was the downside of being on the road. I realized that my afternoon in the office was about to have a downside as well. I'd need to meet with George, or at least touch base with him, then fill Mark in on my progress with the investigation. And there wasn't much to report.

Peggy and Tiffany joined me in my office, armed with coffee and donuts. Tiffany announced that donuts weren't just for breakfast any-more. I liked the way she thought.

It was good to sit down with them. The three of us created a kind of synergy when discussing cases. It helped bring things into focus. Besides, I enjoyed their company. I also enjoyed donuts.

"I'm finished with compiling data, at least for now," Peggy said. "I sifted through police reports and jewelry appraisals. Got rather bug-eyed in the process. No big break-through yet, but hope still springs eternal. Then I decided to change things up, and approach the question from a different angle."

"How so?" It was bound to be something creative. Peggy's mind often worked in mysterious ways.

"The individual police reports weren't very helpful. They were too spread out geographically to be of any use. Then I got to wondering if other insurance companies were seeing the same types of losses as NEC&I. I was pretty sure no companies would share their loss information with us, so I did the next best thing. I began calling police departments noted in our files, not to check on our specific losses, but rather to learn if they had seen a rash of burglaries involving high-end jewelry in their towns."

Good idea. "And how is that going?" I asked.

She shrugged her shoulders. "Nothing specific yet. I'm still waiting to hear back from most of them. In the meantime, I know there has to be some sort of connection among these losses and I intend to find it. Or die trying."

"Don't die, please," I said. "I'm not sure I could manage without you. And I'd hate to have to break in somebody new."

"Gotcha," she replied, as she reached for another donut.

"I have one more chore for you as well, if you feel up to the challenge."

"Always," she said. "What do you need?" She grabbed a pen to make notes.

"See if you can learn anything about the Mullins brothers," I said.

"The who?"

"The Mullins brothers. Tom Foye, from the Foye Agency in Fall River, left me a message asking me to meet him tomorrow so he could tell me all about these folks. I thought they may be a business, but wasn't able to find anything like that online. And Tom sounded desperate to talk about them. I'm eager to hear what he has to say, but I would prefer to show up prepared, if at all possible."

"So do you know anything about these brothers so far?"

I frowned. "Nothing yet. Just their name."

"Can you even give me a hint as to where to start? Do you know where they live? Or what they do?"

I shrugged. "Sorry. I know this is a long shot. Maybe you'll have better luck online than I did. You're good at those things."

"I'll do my best."

"Thanks. Oh, and one more thing."

"I thought you said just one more chore," she said, but smiled as she did so.

"Right. Sorry. Foye wants me to meet him on Block Island. I need to be there a little before noon tomorrow. And I want to get there and back again as quickly as possible. As important as this is, I'll be damned if I'll devote a big chunk of my weekend to it. I need to keep a balance between my job and my life. Can you check out the travel options and figure out the most efficient way for me to get there and back?"

"I'll get right on it," Peggy said. "And good luck with the balance thing. It's nice to see that you've finally figured that out."

"Thanks, I think." I turned to Tiffany. "And what about you? How have your interviews with the underwriting staff been going?" I asked.

She put down her coffee cup. "I'm having a lot of fun."

"Sure," Peggy grinned. "Tiffany gets the easy job. The fun stuff. Gets to sit around drinking coffee and chatting with folks all day while I re-shuffle data on spread-sheets."

"And the nerd in you loves every minute of it," I reminded her.

She nodded. "Guilty as charged. Take it away, Tiffany."

"I've tried to concentrate on the underwriters for the agencies we're actually investigating," Tiffany began. "But I've thrown in just enough of the general population in the department so that my true motives won't be under suspicion."

"That's great," I said. "You'd probably make an excellent spy. So what have you learned?"

She furrowed her brow. "I'll get to that in a minute. First, I have a question. Everybody I spoke with kept talking about CSRs. I know they meant the people who worked in the agencies, but what exactly is a CSR?"

Peggy looked at Tiffany, eyes wide. "You don't know what a CSR is? What are you? New?"

"As a matter of fact, yes I am," Tiffany replied. "So please, just tell me."

I spoke up. "It's short for Customer Service Representative. And a lot easier to say."

"Gotcha. And these CSR people would be the ones who deal with the customers, write coverage, help file claims? Things like that?" she asked.

"Right," I told her. "Now, tell me, did you find anything worth noting or not?"

"I'm not sure."

That, in itself, was intriguing. "Explain yourself, if you please."

"I may be overstating the obvious here, but please remember I'm new to dealing with agents. So far, I've spent much of my time here working with the two of you, and the rest with the ever-popular George. But, the thing I've noticed most is that the majority of the agencies who do business with NEC&I are owned, or run, by men—mostly middle aged or older. And the majority of the worker bees in these offices are women—most of them fairly young."

"And?" I thought I knew where she was going with this, but I wanted to hear it from her.

"Well, does the insurance industry realize that this is the twenty-first century? Women have arrived. They are educated and capable and every bit as competent as men. Or more so in many cases. Glass ceilings are so last millennium."

That made me smile. "We do seem to be a little behind the times in this respect. I'm not sure I know exactly why, but things do seem to change slowly."

Tiffany nodded. "Moving on from that, I wondered how unusual it was to have so many younger women working as CSRs, particularly in our target agencies. So I asked George."

That came as a surprise. "Oh?" I said.

"Yeah. I thought it might be good to make him feel like he was actually involved in this case. He's so much easier to deal with when he's happy. Besides, I wanted to be sure he knew I was working, not just goofing off."

"Good plan," I said. "And what did he say?"

"He said a couple of things." Tiffany referred to her notes. "First of all, he said that CSR positions are entry-level jobs which don't necessarily require a college education. And they pay better than waitressing."

"He may have a point there," Peggy said. "But most agencies do require people to take insurance classes, and to become licensed."

Tiffany looked surprised when she heard that. "That's a relief," she said.

"Did George have any other observations?" I asked.

"He said there's a lot of turnover in personnel in general these days. And that it's just the times we're living in. The twenty-and-thirty-some-thing workers are all eager to move ever-up the corporate ladder. And it seems that job-hopping is the way it's done."

"He may be right about that," I said. I didn't add "for a change," but the look on Peggy's face suggested she heard it anyway.

"Then why are Peggy and I still here?" Tiffany asked.

Peggy decided to answer that. "It's because we're gluttons for punishment."

Tiffany laughed. "Well, whatever the reason, from what I could see, most offices seem to have at least one new employee."

"Is that just our target agencies?" I asked her. "Or in the general population?"

"It seems to be everywhere to some extent. But our target agencies are leading the pack. It's like the entire population of the insurance industry is job-hopping, if you know what I mean. Particularly the younger employees."

My next question was, "Did the underwriters confirm this trend?"

She nodded. "Sure did. And there is something else I found odd."

"What's that?" I asked.

"It's like a big old love-fest going on out there," she said. "The underwriters for the agencies in question absolutely love the customer service folks. They can't say enough good about them. It's almost, like, not normal, if you know what I mean."

Peggy grinned. "You mean that underwriters don't usually have such unbridled affection for agency personnel?"

"Probably not," I told her. "It's more common to hear underwriters complain about their poor-performing agents. Maybe even try to blame the CSRs there for less-than-perfect work. Or for forgetting important details. Or missing information."

Tiffany nodded. "As in people love to gossip. And complain. And cover their own rear ends when something goes wrong."

"Exactly." That struck me as human nature in general, not something specific to the insurance industry. "And what about the agencies in question? Is there no buck-passing there?" I asked.

Tiffany shook her head. "From what I've seen so far, it looks like there is no buck to pass. Everything seems to be perfect."

"So you are telling us that the paperwork and documentation from these agencies is that perfect?" I asked. "That they do a better job than the rest of our agents?"

She nodded. "This is what I've been hearing."

"But that makes no sense," Peggy said. "If that were so, then why would these offices be having the most losses? Not to mention the biggest? You can't believe it's nothing but bad luck."

"Excellent point," I said.

"So where does that leave us?" Tiffany asked.

I gave this some thought. "All things considered, I believe it may be worth looking more deeply into the turnover in our target agencies. Is it simply a sign of the times as George suspects, or is there something else at work here?"

Peggy's eyes lit up. "Like what happened to the old folks they replaced?"

"Excellent point, Peggy." I thought back to something I'd heard the day before. "As a matter of fact, the owner of the Berkshire Insurance Agency told me one of his CSRs died by drowning, when her canoe overturned in a nearby lake. It might be worthwhile to learn what happened to the others. Is this something the two of you could research? Each take half of the agencies in question. Very subtly, of course."

"I can tell you one thing right now," Tiffany said. "Like you asked the other day, I checked into the woman from that agency in Cotuit. The one who had disappeared without a trace a while ago."

I looked up from my notes, eager to hear what would come next.

"Her name was Eleanor Jenkins. Her body was found a couple of weeks ago in a shallow grave by a pond in Marston's Mills. Her throat had been cut."

That was disturbing news. "Oh dear. How dreadful." I thought for a few moments. "OK, here's the plan. I want both of you ladies to work on this idea now. Split up the agencies. Talk to everybody you can about CSRs past and present. Gather as much information as possible on when and why they hired a new CSR. And absolutely find out what happened to the prior employees We know that two of them have died. Maybe the others all retired, or moved away, but you never know. There may be a horrible trend going on here. It's worth looking into."

Chapter 16

It was a little after 1:30 when I finished up with Peggy and Tiffany. I had a 2:00 meeting with Mark to update him on our progress, or lack thereof. I knew I was going to disappoint him. *Bummer.*

The timing was perfect to touch base with George—a necessary evil. I could stop by his office, have a semi-pleasant chat, then tell him I had to leave to see Mark. Planning at its best. I gritted my teeth and marched on.

"Morning, Hotshot," he greeted me. "Long time no see."

"Hello George. How are you? Have you made any progress on our diamond thefts?" Might as well come out swinging. If I put him on the defensive, maybe he wouldn't realize how little progress I was making. I remained standing. At 4'11" I hardly loomed over anybody, but if George stayed seated, I had a slight advantage over him. I'd take whatever I could get.

He glared up at me. "Nothing definitive yet. Still busy sorting the data, comparing our statistics to the current actuarial tables, as well as recent history in the industry as a whole."

"To determine if it's statistically possible that what is happening is actually happening?" I knew I shouldn't have said this. Couldn't resist.

It brought a scowl to his face. "I wouldn't put it exactly that way. However, things are moving more slowly than expected. It seems that Tiffany's social life is getting in the way of her work with me. She is spending more time in the lunchroom than anywhere else. So there you go." He slapped a file folder down on his desk.

"Tiffany is gathering information from the underwriters. Extremely helpful information," I said, though I chose not to go into specifics.

"If you say so, Hotshot. Seems to me it's more like she's having coffee. With everybody. All day. Every day." He snarled in my direction.

"I'm sorry you see it that way," I said.

"I figured you'd say something like that," he sneered. "You've been doing the same thing yourself, all week. Gallivanting all over the state from what I heard. 'Interviewing agents.'" He air quoted this last bit. "What I don't understand is why you haven't put these agents on official notice that they're about to be terminated. You should have started with that."

"No way," I responded. "If we did that, they'd have no reason to work with us on this. We need their cooperation."

George glowered at me. "Give me a break. Do you think they're going to admit their problems? Or confess their crimes and turn themselves in? And while you're out there socializing, your work here isn't getting done. And I bet you're no closer to finding answers than I am." He folded his arms across his chest and glared at me.

I stared him down—one of my better tricks. "Don't be so sure."

"Oh? Do you have something to report?"

"I think Tiffany, Peggy and I may be on to something. Listen, I'd love to chat more with you about this case but I've got a 2:00 meeting with Mark. To fill him in on things. After all, I do report to him." *Like you report to me.* "Keep me posted on your progress." I made a semi-graceful exit and headed for the stairs.

Mark was on the phone when I arrived. He held up one finger and motioned for me to sit.

I complied.

He completed his call a few moments later. "Good to see you Amy. How's the investigation going?"

I gave him the low-down on what Peggy, Tiffany and I were checking into. I didn't mention the Mullins brothers yet. It would be better to have more information before broaching that subject.

"Interesting," he said. "You may just be onto something. What does George think?"

I shrugged.

Mark frowned. "You didn't discuss this with him, did you?"

"Not yet," I admitted.

"Because ...?" Mark's entire face signaled his disappointment.

"Because it wouldn't help. I can explain to him why we're doing what we're doing. But I can't understand it for him. I believe he's taking the wrong approach, but I don't want to fight with him. Sometimes it's important to know when to stop arguing with people and simply let them be wrong."

"I get what you're saying," Mark sighed. "But you're going to have to fill him in eventually. Please make it sooner rather than later." He gave me his stern "I'm your boss. Do what I say" look. I pretended not to notice.

Our meeting ended on that note. I promised to keep Mark in the loop and returned to my office intending to catch up on some paperwork.

Peggy greeted me with a lopsided grin. "I've got the info you wanted."

"On the Mullins brothers?" *That was fast.*

She shook her head. "Sorry, no. Not yet. But I have figured out Block Island."

"And?"

"There's a ferry that goes from Fall River. High speed. It's a two-and-a-half-hour trip."

Yikes! "That's high speed?" I asked. "How can it possibly take that long? The place is just off the coast of Rhode Island."

"I know what you mean, but I'm afraid that's the deal," she said. "You can also get the ferry at Point Judith, but that's a two-hour ride from Cambridge—on a good day."

"I'd have to leave at the crack of dawn to get to the ferry in order to meet Tom Foye at noon."

"There is an alternative," Peggy said.

"Oh?"

"You can fly there. From Westerly, Rhode Island. It's a twelve-minute flight."

"Sounds quick, but most likely costly." I had to worry about my expense account. Times were tight at NEC&I.

"Not too bad," Peggy said. "Round trip under $120. I took the liberty of booking you a flight at 11:30. You can get a cab from the airport into town.

Here's the info on two cab companies." She handed me a sticky note with two telephone numbers.

"How far is Westerly from here?" I asked. Something told me she would have checked on that as well. Peggy was nothing if not efficient.

"Nearly 100 miles from Cambridge," she announced. "But only 70 miles from Massapoag Junction. Your best bet is to stay with Pete tonight. If you leave his place between 9:30 and 10:00, you'll make the flight just fine."

Peggy was right of course. It only made sense to leave from Pete's new home in the morning. I had mixed emotions as I called him to discuss my change of plans. Here I was trying not to get too comfortable with staying there. I wasn't ready to make that leap yet. It was important for me to maintain my own space, my own life, not simply morph into Pete's. On the other hand, I didn't want to lose him. And I did want him to be happy. I hated being so conflicted. Nevertheless, I made the call.

"Ames, hi," he said. "Funny. I was just going to call you."

Something in his voice sounded slightly off. "About what?" I asked.

"Why don't you go first? After all, you called me."

There was definitely something going on with him. I hurried to explain my upcoming trip to Block Island.

"Of course you can stay here. Any time you want. You know that," he said. "I love having you here."

And I loved being there, just not all the time. Not yet. "Would you like to come to Block Island with me?" I asked. "After all, tomorrow is Saturday. It could be fun."

"I wish I could. I've never been there. But I've got to spend some time at the office tomorrow. Getting organized. And familiarizing myself with the files."

"Didn't you do that today?" I asked. That had been his plan.

"I made a good start at it," he said. "Then I went home for lunch and the day went sideways from there."

"What do you mean?"

"I got home to discover that someone that had broken into my house. And I was robbed." He choked audibly on that last word.

"Robbed? Pete, that's awful. Are you all right?"

He let out a weary-sounding sigh. "I'll be fine."

The tone of his voice told me otherwise, but it was better to let him pretend to be stoic for a while. "Did they do much damage? Or take much?"

"They destroyed the lock to the front door. I spent half of the afternoon dealing with that. And the other half filling out a police report and speaking with the insurance company. They'll probably cancel me for filing a claim when the policy is less than a week old."

"We can worry about that later. So, tell me, what was taken?" While Pete had nice enough things, I wasn't sure most of it was worth stealing.

"As far as I can tell, just one thing. My mother's engagement ring. I can't believe it's gone."

I heard the hint of a sob in his voice, something I seldom heard from him. *Oh dear. Not his mother's ring. The ring he chose not to keep in a safe deposit box. The ring I was afraid he might try to give to me before I was ready for it. But now was not the time to say all that.* "I'm so sorry, Pete. I know how much that ring means to you."

"At least I already got it added to my new insurance policy. They were willing to take the old appraisal, even though it's hopelessly out of date," he said. "They gave me one month to get a new appraisal. And instead, I'm filing a claim. I wish I'd put my policy with NEC&I." His voice became steadier as he discussed the business end of things.

"Was anything else taken?" I asked.

"I'm not sure yet. Whoever was here sure did ransack the place. It'll take me a while to sort it all out."

"Not to worry about that. I'll help you—with your house and your claim. We'll deal with it one thing at a time." I felt the walls closing in around me. Pete's being burglarized was more than upsetting. It was disturbing on a whole new level. There was no way this was a coincidence. But I wouldn't add to Pete's troubles by mentioning that at this time. Right now, he was upset. He needed me. And I would be there for him. At the same time, I needed to learn what Tom Foye had to tell me—and why he had sounded so frightened. I needed to find a way to deal with it all. And quickly.

Something told me my weekend was about to go seriously down the tubes.

Chapter 17

I dashed home to pack a bag and pick up Sam. We then spent over an hour in traffic on our way to Pete's. And I worried about Pete the entire time. My usually even-tempered, upbeat guy had sounded badly stressed on the phone. Not at all himself. I needed to give him all the love and attention I could this evening. I would worry about Tom Foye later.

Pete was waiting in his front yard when I arrived. He looked beyond upset over the theft of his mother's ring. I gave him a big bear hug.

"I'm glad you're here, Ames," he said. "It's been one hell of a horrible day. Let's get out of here for a while. Go someplace where I can get myself a good stiff drink and get my mind off my troubles."

"Sure thing. But I'm driving. How about that funny little Irish restaurant in the strip mall? They serve comfort food, which is what we need at the moment."

"Works for me."

Café Begorrah was nearly as empty as the last time we were there. Mostly unoccupied tables. The same waitress. And the same man sitting at a corner table. With the same sour expression on his face. He wasn't alone tonight, though. A youngish fellow in a leather jacket and clunky army boots was with him. They were huddled over a laptop, deep enough in conversation that they didn't look up when Pete and I arrived.

"Evening, folks," the waitress closed the book she had been studying and greeted us. "It's nice to see you again. Please sit anywhere you like. I'll be right over with menus for you."

We sat by the window again. Pete ordered a double scotch; I preferred a glass of Pinot Noir. When our drinks arrived, I raised my glass. "My poor Pete," I said. "You have had quite a week. What with moving, then learning your new insurance agent was murdered, then being burglarized, you must be ready to scream."

He shook his head. "I've already done that. It didn't help. I'll be all right, Ames. Not to worry. I'll pull myself together. I always do. Besides, there were a few good things in the week as well. I'd rather talk about them right now. It will help me to remain positive."

"Nice idea. Tell me what was good." I took his hand and gave him my full attention.

He smiled. "Other than the time I spent with you, you mean? That's always good. Let's see ... before it all went to Hell, I touched base with the Easton Youth Baseball folks the other day. And signed up to work with them, on a volunteer basis."

"Doing what?"

"I'm not sure yet. Maybe coaching, or keeping score, or working the concession stand. Whatever needs doing."

"You'll enjoy that, won't you?"

He smiled. "Sure will. I'll love working with the kids. I also connected with the local food pantry. I'll be working with them one afternoon a week."

And this was why I loved the guy. They simply didn't come any nicer.

"Did you put much time in at your new office?" I asked.

"Sure did. I've begun looking over the client files. And I also got my first case."

"Oh? Anything intriguing?"

"Yes and no," he said.

"Explain, please."

"A fellow came in. The son of a client. His father passed away, before I even had a chance to meet the guy. Fortunately my predecessor kept his files in good order. I located the will with no problem."

"Will you be handling the estate now?" I asked.

He nodded. "And with any luck, maybe I can do some estate work for the son as well. We chatted about the need for a plan—a will, a power-of-attorney, etc. He seemed to take to the idea. I guess that means my practice is already growing."

"Where there's a will, there's a way," I said, unable to resist.

"Please tell me you didn't just say that," he groaned.

"Sorry." Pete hated bad puns almost as much as I loved them.

The waitress came by to take our orders. This time Pete went for the shepherd's pie and I chose the beef stew. Comfort food was just what we both needed after a busy, rough week.

When our meals arrived, I asked the waitress, "How are your studies going? Are you learning a lot about insurance?"

She grimaced. "Right. Just passed the license exam. I guess that's a good thing, even if it is boring beyond belief."

"Then why do it?" Pete asked.

"I've got to do something with my life" she shrugged. "Can't make a living here."

I couldn't argue with that.

"And I've got a new job as well," she continued. "Starting Monday. This is my last night here. Lord knows I'll be glad to see the last of the place. The only good thing about it is that it's close to where I live."

"Moira!" the man at the corner table snarled to her. "Get over here."

"Oops," she said. "Gotta go. Enjoy your meals."

"Good luck with the new job," I said as she hurried off to speak with her boss. Anything would be better than dealing with that guy on a regular basis.

Pete and I dug into our dinners in companionable silence. That was one of the best things about our relationship. We were both okay with the quiet times.

After a while, Pete looked around the restaurant and shook his head. "You've got to wonder how this place survives. Here it is the beginning of the weekend and we're almost the only customers here."

I pondered that for a moment. "Maybe that's not what this place is about. Maybe it serves another purpose."

"What purpose might that be?" he asked. "And this better be good."

"How about money laundering?"

Pete gave me an indulgent smile. "I do love the way your mind works, Ames. Don't always understand it, but I love it anyway."

I swallowed the last of my wine in one final gulp

"Want another?" Pete asked.

I shook my head. "We better get going. I need to make this an early night. I have a busy day tomorrow. I only hope whatever it is Tom Foye wants to discuss with me is worth the trip to Block Island.

Chapter 18

Peggy had been spot-on with my travel arrangements. The ride from Pete's house to the airport in Westerly was a breeze on a Saturday morning. I arrived in plenty of time for the flight, which I shared with two other passengers. It took exactly twelve minutes, just as Peggy had said. During that short time, the cabin attendant informed me that Block Island was nine miles off the Rhode Island Coast, was primarily a summer tourist destination and had a year-round population of just over one thousand residents. I figured it must be a quiet place off-season. My fellow passengers, both good-looking young men in jeans and sweatshirts, appeared oblivious to this travelogue. Maybe they already knew these things. Maybe they didn't care. Maybe they weren't quite awake yet.

It was a short cab ride from the airport to downtown Block Island, barely a mile. I didn't get to see much of the local scenery. From what I did see, I guessed it was quaint and charming in the summer. And the scent of salt air was always a treat. Still, on this gray early spring day, the island appeared rather bleak. It also appeared deserted; there was nary a soul in sight. That was fine with me. My current concern was with Tom Foye. I was antsy and anxious to learn what he wanted to tell me about the Mullins brothers. And why our conversation had to be so clandestine. I felt like I was living in a bad spy novel.

My cab arrived in what passed for the center of town a few minutes before noon and pulled up in front of Dead Eye Dick's. There was some sort of commotion across the street—emergency vehicles, police, EMTs and a few dozen curious on-lookers. This both surprised and alarmed me. A cold shiver made its way up my spine. Was this merely a coincidence, or did it somehow involve Tom Foye? I paid the cab and dashed into the restaurant. Maybe someone in there could fill me in on what was going on.

A skinny young man with a handlebar mustache greeted me. "Table for one?" he asked.

"Actually two. I'm meeting someone for lunch."

He showed me to a table by the front window. "Can I get you something while you wait?" he asked.

"Just a cup of coffee for now," I told him, then asked, "Do you know what all that ruckus is about across the street?"

"They've been there all morning," he told me. "Somebody passed away at the inn."

Holy shit! This was not a good sign! Please don't let it be Tom Foye!

"Sorry. Gotta dash," the waiter said as another customer appeared at the door.

I attempted to question him further when he delivered my coffee, but the lunch crowd, small as it was, began to arrive and demand his attention. I concentrated on the scene across the street, watching the police hold back the curious townsfolks as the ambulance took off down the street. And trying to keep my imagination in check. Not an easy thing to do. My gut somehow knew that it was all about Tom Foye. There was, after all, no such thing as coincidence.

A short while later, my coffee was cold, the aroma of bacon cooking was making my stomach churn and there was still no sign of Tom Foye. I was beyond worried.

The waiter returned, with a look of pity on his face, as if he thought I'd been stood up by a blind date or something equally awkward and embarrassing.

"Are you ready to order?" he asked.

I shook my head. "No, thanks, but I do have a question. Do you know Tom Foye?" *And please tell me that wasn't him in that ambulance.*

His eyes grew wide. "Is that who you've been waiting for? Tom Foye?"

"Yes it is."

The waiter gave me a solemn look. "I don't know quite how to tell you this, but I'm afraid Tom won't be joining you for lunch. That was him in the ambulance."

My worst fears were confirmed. The coffee cup jumped out of my hand and shattered as it hit the table, spreading a puddle of coffee in its wake. "What happened to him? How did he die? And when?" *And does that mean I will never learn what Tom needed to tell me about the Mullins brothers? Were they responsible for this? If so, why would they want him dead?* That wasn't fair. Karma wasn't supposed to work that way.

The waiter frowned. "I can't tell you much of anything. All I know is that when I came in to open for breakfast this morning, the EMTs were bringing Tom's body out on a stretcher and into an ambulance."

"Was he dead at that point?" I asked.

"I think so." The waiter told me. "They had him in in a body bag, but it wasn't closed all the way. I could see the top of his head. And I'm pretty sure there had been foul play of some sort."

Damn! This was getting worse by the minute. "What makes you say that?"

"The police have been there all morning."

"That doesn't necessarily indicate foul play," I told him. "The scene of an unattended or unexpected death is always treated like a crime scene. Until or unless it is proven otherwise."

"And his head was covered with blood," he added.

I bit my tongue so I wouldn't say anything rude. One would think the man could have started with that fact. Sometimes it's hard to figure people.

"And that's all I know," he told me. "The police haven't let anybody anywhere near the inn. Not even that news reporter. You know, the guy from WJAR." He pointed across the street. "See. There he is with his camera man. Packing up their gear."

I looked across and saw the two fellows who'd been on the plane with me. I thanked the waiter and headed across the street.

A young policeman with curly blond hair and a snarl on his lips stopped me on the sidewalk. "Sorry, Ma'am. I can't let you go any further."

"I understand that," I told him. "I really do. But this is an important part of an investigation I'm conducting. I need to know what happened here."

"Is that so?" He shrugged. "Are you some kind of cop?"

"Insurance investigator," I replied. I handed him my card.

He shook his head, apparently unimpressed by my credentials. "Insurance, huh? Boy you people sure do move fast. That poor guy has only been dead a couple of hours. Isn't it kind of soon to be dealing with his life insurance? Sorry. You still can't go in there."

I didn't bother to correct the cop about the insurance. "Is there anybody I could speak with about what happened?"

He pointed to an older man in a police uniform standing by the door to the inn scowling. "Bob's in charge. But I doubt he'll tell you anything."

I marched toward the door. It didn't help. Bob wouldn't even acknowledge my presence. I stood on the sidewalk silently fretting and fuming and wondering what my next move should be. I scanned the sidewalk for the news reporters. They were heading into Dead Eye Dick's. I decided to join them.

"Hello," I said as I approached their table. "Would you gentlemen mind if I joined you? I'd like to ask you a few questions if I may."

The camera guy shrugged and pulled out his cell phone.

The reporter gave me a quizzical look. He had dark wavy hair and the most gorgeous blue eyes. "Weren't you on the plane with us this morning?"

"Yes I was. You know, I thought you looked familiar. I was pretty preoccupied. What's your name again?" I hoped this sounded more convincing to him than it did to me. Sometimes I'm not the greatest liar.

He smiled. "I'm Chris Farmer. WJAR news. Have a seat."

I sat. My guess was that Chris Farmer must be the new guy to merit an early Saturday morning assignment like this on a nearly-deserted island.

The waiter arrived. We all ordered coffee.

"This is my cameraman Jerry Greene," Chris said.

Jerry acknowledged my presence, flashed a phony smile in my general direction and returned his attention to his cell phone.

"My name is Amy Lynch. I'm a friend of Tom Foye's. I was supposed to meet him here for lunch," I said. I didn't offer them my card. Didn't want to set off any alarms concerning the reason for my lunch date. Better to let them think I had a thing for older, overweight men than to have them suspect there might be a bigger story here. The last thing I needed today was to end up on the 6:00 PM news, even if it was in Rhode Island. With the way my luck had been running lately, whoever had murdered Tom Foye would see it and come after me. Not a risk I was willing to take.

The fellow with the camera remained glued to his phone. The reporter was less rude. "So you and the deceased were friends? I'm sorry for your loss."

I was sorry too.

The reporter's eyes lit up. "Maybe you could give me some background info on the deceased," he said.

Oh dear. I didn't want to have to lie to an investigative reporter. "I didn't know him very well. We only met each other recently. He owns an insurance agency in Fall River." That was all true. Now was a good time to change the subject. "The police wouldn't tell me anything. Were you able to learn what happened to Tom?"

He gave me a small smile. "I did manage to speak with the chambermaid before the cops spirited her away. She told me she went to make up Tom's room this morning. She knocked on his door. When he didn't respond, she assumed he was out and let herself in with her pass key. She found him bleeding on the floor. And that's all I know. Like I said, sorry."

At the risk of appearing pushy, I continued to question the guy. "Do you know where they took the body?"

"I'm guessing the hospital in Westerly."

"Would the Westerly police become involved then?" I asked.

"I suppose," he said. "I'll do a some of research when I get back to the station. Watch me on the evening news. I should know more by then."

I smiled. I would indeed watch the news. Right now, that seemed to be the best, if not the only, way to get more information. And I needed to know who killed Tom Foye. Also why. Our coffee arrived.

"Drink up quick," Farmer said to his co-worker. "We need to get back out there and see what we can learn from the locals. See if we can get a couple of quotes, perhaps film some local color, such as it is this time of year." He turned to me. "We'll probably see you on the flight back."

The assistant picked up his cup and drained it in a few quick gulps.

After the newsmen left, I grabbed my phone and called Peggy's number at the office. My intention was to leave her a message. She surprised me by answering the phone.

"What in the world are you doing there on a Saturday?" I asked.

"Just catching up on a few things. No big deal. So what's up?"

I needed to talk to someone. And Peggy was willing to listen. Speaking softly into my phone so as not to be overheard, I poured my heart out to her in response to her question. Pete's robbery. Tom Foye's death. My growing discomfort with this case.

Peggy listened without interrupting. When I was all talked out, she said, "It is all dreadful, that's for sure. But hang in there. You'll get it all worked out eventually. You always do."

I sat staring out the window of Dead Eye Dick's. I had nearly an hour before my return flight and decided to spend it people watching. There weren't all that many people on Block Island this time of year. But one of them was a murderer. I shook off the chill that thought gave me. I needed to gather my wits about me. Fast. Tom Foye's killer was out there some-where. So far the waiter and the newsmen were the only people who knew I came to the island to meet with Tom. I preferred to keep it that way. Just in case. In case what, I wasn't sure, but I wasn't taking any chances.

Chapter 19

Part of me wanted to pick Sam up at Pete's, visit for a while, then head back to Cambridge. I had things I needed to do on Sunday—laundry, shopping and the like, the basic necessities of life. I was looking forward to having them distract me for a while. Now there was no way any of that was going to happen. My household chores would have to wait—probably until I ran out of clean underwear. I didn't want to be alone at the moment. Tom Foye's death had shaken me up. I needed to push that out of my head for a while, along with the elusive Mullins brothers, whoever they may be.

Most importantly, Pete needed me right now. And I would never let him down. I needed him as much as he needed me, a thought that both comforted and terrified me. On the other hand, I was beginning to wonder if being strong and independent wasn't all it was cracked up to be.

Pete suggested dinner out again. I declined, preferring pizza delivery. "I need to watch the Rhode Island evening news to see what I can learn about Tom Foye's death," I told him.

"Good idea," Pete said, but he looked disappointed. I had to find a way to fix that, one way or another.

"You know, Pete, I think we both need to take a day off tomorrow. Do something fun. How does that sound?"

"Works for me. It'd be good to get my mind off my troubles. Any idea what you'd like to do?"

I shook my head. "Give me some time. I'll come up with something."

I was up at the crack of dawn Sunday morning after a miserable night's sleep. There was far too much going on in my head, and none of it was good. The Rhode Island evening news had made a big deal about Tom Foye's murder. Local insurance agent murdered. Blunt force trauma. First murder on Block Island in over twenty years. No apparent motive. Killer at large. Sensational news. Also mostly things I already knew.

There was a possible suspect the police were trying to locate. The only "stranger" at the inn that weekend. A forty-something man of average height, average weight and dark brown hair. The hotel clerk said the man had something funny about one of his eyes and that he had checked in under the name David Jones. He appeared to have left the island, though not by ferry or plane. The only alternative I could come up with was a private boat. Not very helpful.

The story replayed itself over and over in my dreams, leaving me groggy and sleep-deprived. I definitely needed a day off. But what to do?

Then I had an idea. I got up and went to work on it right away and by the time Pete was up, everything was all set.

"Don't linger too long over your coffee," I said to him. "It's supposed to be nice weather today and I have a fun day planned for us. It will do us both good."

"Anything would be more fun than the last few days," he said. "So what's the plan?"

"We're going on a picnic."

He thought that over. "Sounds fine so far. Shall I get to work packing a lunch?"

I shook my head. "Lunch is all set. We'll have to bring our own wine, though. And be discreet about it. It's technically not allowed where we're going, but if we put it in a thermos nobody will know. I ordered the rest from Joe's Diner up the street. Sandwiches and salad. And chocolate chip cookies. We can pick everything up on our way."

"On our way where?" he asked.

"Dighton Rock State Park," I announced. "In Berkley."

"Hmmm. And what is the attraction there?"

"A rock, of course."

Pete grinned at me. "I should have seen that one coming. Tell me more."

"Dighton Rock is an archaeological oddity. A mystery from the past. I've always wanted to see it. It's in a museum now, in the park of the same name. The museum's open by appointment only. They're expecting us at 11:00. It's not far from here, just off Route 24 South. We should leave in half an hour or so." *And I won't even think about my investigation today. No Mullins brothers. No deceased Tom Foye. Just me and Pete enjoying our time together. Pulling that off won't be easy, but I will find a way to make it happen. Or I'll fake it if I have to.*

"You have had a busy morning, haven't you?" he grinned. "Guess I better hit the shower so we can get on the road on time."

My Pete was in much better shape than the past few days. That was a relief.

Forty minutes later, we were in the car, picnic lunch and thermos of contraband wine stowed discreetly in the trunk. As we exited Route 24 onto a more rural road, Pete checked the sky and frowned. "I thought you said we'd have nice weather today. You may have been misinformed. Those sure look like rain clouds to me."

I shook my head. "Not to worry. We'll be fine."

"How do you know that?"

I pointed to the farmland on the left. "See those cows. They're all standing up."

"Don't they usually?"

"Not always," I replied. "When it's going to rain, they all sit down on the ground."

That got a laugh out of Pete. "Is that so? I imagine that's something your mother told you, right?"

"Right. And, see that patch of blue sky off to the left? She told me about that too. She said that if there's enough blue in the sky to make a Dutchman's pants, it's going to clear up."

Pete gave me a funny look but didn't comment on that. Wisely so.

A few minutes later, we arrived at Dighton Rock State Park. The sign informed us that it was ninety-eight acres large. It was also peaceful, with an abundance of green grass and trees. Hopefully the very thing to help the two of us relax.

The museum was a small white building overlooking the Taunton River. We parked just outside and approached the building. Before we could knock on the door, it opened and a tiny gnome-like lady appeared. She was shorter than me by at least two inches, making her somewhere around four foot nine, and had a head full of tight gray curls. She wore a mid-calf length denim skirt, an embroidered peasant blouse and sensible, aka extremely ugly, shoes. "Good morning," she said with an over-sized smile. "I'm Gertrude Meyers, the assistant state archaeologist here. Please just call me Gertie."

Pete shook her outstretched hand. "Nice to meet you, Gertie."

"Yes," I added. "We're so pleased that you were able to meet with us here on such short notice. We're eager to learn about the rock."

"Not a problem," she said. "I was delighted when you called this morning. I didn't have other plans for the day and I do love showing our rock to visitors. Please come this way."

We followed her inside to view the main attraction. It was large, grayish-brown and covered with unusual carvings.

"Dighton Rock is five feet high, eleven feet long and weighs about forty tons," Gertie told us.

Pete approached the rock for a close-up inspection. "Where was it found?" he asked.

"Not far from here. In the Taunton River, in the town of Dighton. It was moved here in 1963 to preserve it from further erosion."

"What can you tell us about its history?" I asked. "Do we know who did the carvings? Or why?"

Gertie began her spiel. "It dates back prior to 1680. That's when the first mention of it showed up in print, by a fellow named John Danforth. And ever since then, it has been the subject of all manner of theories and speculations."

"Speculation as to who made these drawings?" Pete asked.

Gertie nodded. "And also as to what they were trying to depict."

I took a long hard look at the designs on the rock. "These carvings aren't like anything else I've ever seen. They appear to be more pictographs than any sort of alphabet."

"Not like that Celtic language you told me about," Pete said. "That appeared to be a fairly complex system. This is more like Egyptian hiero-glyphics," he added. "Only different. Simpler. Less sophisticated."

I agreed with that. "What do you know about the origins of these carvings?" I asked Gertie.

"Over the years, it has been suggested that they were done by local indigenous people, Viking visitors, Phoenicians, the Chinese, the Portuguese."

"What?" Pete asked. "No mention of aliens?"

"Of course there was," Gertie laughed. "I'm inclined to dismiss that theory."

"What do you think?" I asked.

"I tend to ascribe to Occam's razor. You know, the idea that when presented with a variety of theories on a given subject, the simplest idea is most likely the correct one. Which means I suspect the carvings were done by the local indigenous people."

"I think I'd have to agree with you there," Pete said.

Gertie nodded. "Though for what purpose, I have no idea. I hope we figure it out one of these days."

We spent some time checking out the documents on display discussing the history of the rock, then thanked Gertie and retrieved our picnic basket from the car.

I looked up at the sky and smiled. It was clear blue now, not a trace of clouds. "See," I said to Pete. "My mother was right."

He laughed and walked toward a picnic table overlooking the river. A quiet, pleasant spot to enjoy our lunch. I set out the food and poured us each a paper cup of wine. "So, tell me, what did you think?"

"I think I'm beginning to understand your interest in archaeology," he told me. "Perhaps even share it. It also reminded me to hang my house-warming gift on the front door. What did you call that language?"

"Ogham."

Pete smiled at me. "Thanks again for the welcome sign. And also for planning this day. Lord knows I needed it."

As did I. I only hoped it would help me pull myself together enough to put a stop to the diamond thefts before they got the better of all of us at NEC&I.

Chapter 20

Our day off and excursion to Dighton Rock did both Pete and me a world of good. Fresh air and sunshine were good for the soul as well as the body. We both slept like the dead Sunday night. I had intended to return to Cambridge Sunday evening, always wary of giving Pete the mistaken notion that I was ready to move to Massapoag Junction. In the end, though, I was too weary to drive. We had a pleasant, cozy evening. Sam and I left early the next morning.

Pushing myself back into working mode, I obsessed about Tom Foye's murder all the way to Cambridge. I needed to talk with the police. I'd deal with that later, though. I had to work out why it had happened and how it affected my case. I needed to put it out of my mind for a while though, so I wouldn't make myself crazy. Sometimes my best simply wasn't good enough.

I had an appointment at the Ross Insurance Agency in Newton, just outside of Boston, at 10:00. That gave me plenty of time to bring Sam home to Cambridge and get him settled in for the day, then shower and change. I reviewed my files over a second cup of coffee. The Ross Agency was somewhat of a wild card for NEC&I. While they had been in business for years, they were new to us. We had signed them on only two years ago, so they didn't have much of an actual track record. An in-person visit should give us an idea of what to expect from them in the future—or not.

I jumped into my Mustang and headed for Newton. I touched base with Peggy on the way, rehashing my disastrous trip to Block Island with her. "Please see if you can learn anything more about this," I said. "It doesn't sit well with me when somebody with supposedly important information for us suddenly ends up dead."

"Will do," she told me.

"Thanks. I'll see you later."

The drive to Newton was easy enough, but parking was a bear. I realized only too late that public transportation may have been the better choice.

Parking my car on a side street, I walked the several blocks to the Ross Agency. That was all right by me. It was a pleasant morning. The exercise felt good. My destination was a small store-front office in the center of town. Both Valentine's Day and St. Patrick's Day decorations still hung in the windows. Not a good sign in mid-April. I took a deep breath and opened the door.

A middle-aged man in a slightly crumpled gray suit greeted me. "Good morning. I'm David Ross. Are you Ms. Lynch?"

"I am. It's nice to meet you." I wasn't yet sure if that was true, but social convention dictated that I say it. I handed him my card. "How are you doing this morning?"

Ross ran his fingers through what remained of his gray-brown hair. "I've had better days I'm afraid, but we'll muddle through somehow."

Oh dear. That didn't bode well at all. "Is there a problem?" I asked, not at all eager to hear the answer.

He stared at his shoes. "It's just that ... well ... I'm afraid I haven't been able to locate the files you wanted to discuss. The only information I was able to find was from the NEC&I website. I believe that's all stuff you already know. We don't pay much attention to paper files these days, since we can get most of what we need through your website."

"Oh? I see," I responded. I took a deep breath to keep my temper in check as I waited for him to continue.

"Right," he said, avoiding my eyes. "I spent most of yesterday trying to locate the paper files. Even came in early this morning to give it another go. I'm sorry to say, I've had no luck."

I was tempted to ask if he had trouble with the alphabet—since most offices files are arranged that way—but bit my tongue. "Do you mean to tell me that some of the files I requested are missing?"

"They all are," he replied as he slumped into a chair.

I had no idea how to respond to that. *Was it actually possible that NEC&I was dealing with an agent who couldn't even locate his own paper files?*

"You see," he began, "Louise, who worked for me for years, had her own filing system. I could never figure it out, but that didn't matter, because she was always there to help me. I dealt with the clients and she handled the paperwork, as well as the computer input. And she always knew where everything was. God, I miss her."

I stood there staring at the man. I wondered where Louise was now. "Did you hire a replacement for Louise?" *And does she know the alphabet?*

"I did. A fine girl. Sharp as a tack. Her name is Maggie. She has spent the past couple of months trying to re-organize the office. And she's doing a fine job of it so far. But this is a busy place. She doesn't always have much time for the clerical part of things. Helping the clients is far more important to us. She concentrates on that."

I could accept that philosophy in general, but wondered how much help Maggie could provide without the customer files. "Did Maggie try to locate the files?"

Ross shook his head. "Sorry. No. She wasn't here yesterday. It was her birthday. I gave her the day off. Lord knows she deserved it. The girl is an absolute treasure. Always cheerful, always helpful. The clients love her."

"And where is she today?" I asked.

He looked at his watch and shook his head. "Running somewhat late for some reason. I don't know why. It's never happened before in all the months she's been here." He let out a noisy sigh. "So, tell me, how much trouble am I in? I mean, is there a problem with the claims you want to discuss? Are you suspecting fraud or something? Please tell me it's nothing like that."

"You're not in any trouble," I told him. *At least not yet.* "We don't suspect anything at the moment. We're looking into some burglary claims with a number of agencies. It appears we may have a jewel thief on the loose, with a particular fondness for fine diamonds. We're hoping our agents, yourself included, might be able to help us sort this out."

"I'd be glad to," he said. "What do you need to know? I'll see what I can remember."

Willing to try anything, I pulled my files out of my briefcase. "What can you tell me about Michael and Evelyn Curtin?"

Ross smiled. "Good people. They've been with me for ages. Funny, though, I don't recall Evie having any special jewelry coverage. Was it something valuable that was lost?"

"A diamond solitaire, worth over forty thousand dollars," I said.

His eyes popped. "Forty thousand dollars? Wouldn't you think I'd remember insuring something that valuable? Hmmm. Maybe Louise handled that."

So far not very helpful. I grabbed my next file. "What about Alicia Duncan? What can you tell me about her?"

"Very nice woman. A widow. Her husband Will died a few years ago. He was a great guy. But I've got to tell you, I don't remember them having any expensive jewelry either."

Maybe Louise had handled that as well. "What about Larry Solnik?"

"Larry's an old bachelor. I've known him forever. Salt of the earth, he is. It's hard to imagine him with any expensive jewelry, though. I guess you just never know about people."

And on it went. David Ross apparently knew his clients well on a personal basis, but was not at all familiar with the particulars of their insurance coverage. It appeared that Louise must have handled all the actual insurance business that went on here. I wondered what David Ross did with his time. "In general, who takes care of writing coverage here?" I asked.

"Bringing in new business is my job."

"And once the business is on the books, who services the policy if changes are needed?"

"That was Louise's job. Now Maggie handles it."

"And who deals with the claims?"

"Same thing. I used to do all that, when I first started up. Then I got older, and my wife got sick, and I left more and more of the detail work here to my employees."

That was not what I wanted to hear. I was about to give up when the front door flew open and a breathless young woman bounded in. She was tall and thin, with raven-black hair that could only be described as thick and luxurious. Most women would kill for hair like that. She wore tight blue jeans torn at the knees and a lavender cashmere sweater. I was surprised that jeans were allowed in the office, but it was none of my business.

"So sorry I'm late, Dave," she said. "Believe it or not, I over-slept. That never happens to me. I guess I must've partied too much last night, it being my birthday and all. I promise it won't happen again."

Ross gave her an indulgent smile. "Not to worry, Maggie. You're forgiven. I was young once myself, you know."

Maggie hung her coat on a hook. "So what's going on here?" she asked, looking at me.

"This is Amy Lynch from New England Casualty and Indemnity," Ross told her.

Before he could continue, Maggie broke in. "See what my boyfriend Mike gave me for my birthday." She held out her left arm to display a silver bracelet.

"May I see?" I asked in an effort to appear friendly—far friendlier than I was feeling at the moment. She thrust her arm in my general direction. It was quite a lovely bracelet, but I had far more important things on my mind.

Apparently Ross wasn't much interested in silver jewelry. "Ms. Lynch wants to discuss some burglary claims with us. Sad to say, I haven't been able to find the files."

"Claim files?" she asked. "I can probably get those for you." She sat at a desk and opened a bottom drawer. "Names?"

"Let's start with Curtin, Duncan and Solnik," I said.

"Sure thing." She rustled through the drawer for a few moments then placed three manila file folders on her desk.

I was appalled. "That's where you keep your claim files? In your desk drawer?"

Maggie lowered her eyes. "Only until I find the actual file folders where they belong. I'm still working on getting those organized logically. It's quite a challenge, you know. I've been here just over a year now and have barely made any progress at all. Too many other things to do. More important things."

"Like what?" I asked.

"Clients are always my first priority," she said. "Helping them in any way I can. It's what I love about this job. The clerical stuff I attack in the quiet moments." She sighed. "And there haven't been a lot of those lately. David and I are both putting in a lot of extra time, but not making much progress yet."

So it would seem, much to my dismay.

Maggie looked at the top claim file. "Alicia Duncan. I remember when she came in to report this claim. Poor woman was devastated. The diamond that was stolen was a fiftieth anniversary gift from her husband Will. He's gone now. She's desperately lonely without him."

"May I take a look at those?" I asked, pointing to the paperwork on her desk.

"Help yourself."

As I reached for the files, David Ross cleared his throat noisily. "Ah, if you ladies would excuse me, I'll be in my office for a while. I have a few calls I need to return before lunch time. Knock if you need anything." And off he went.

"Sure thing," Maggie told him.

I said nothing, just sat studying the paperwork Maggie had given me. It was a major disappointment, absolutely nothing there that we didn't have in the claim files at our office. I was having mixed feelings about this agency. While their overall organization was a mess, they definitely had a good handle on their clients. I'd report all this to their underwriter and let him, or her, decide how to deal with things. Not my job!

"We'd like to see the entire client files, underwriting information and all," I said to Maggie. "If I give you a list of the clients in question, would you be good enough to locate them for me?"

She smiled. "I can't promise I'll find them, but I'll do my very best."

Hoping that her very best would be good enough, I stood to leave. No point wasting any more time here. "I'd appreciate it," I said, handing her a list of names. "Please call me when they're ready. I guess I'll say good-bye to Mr. Ross and be on my way for now."

Maggie looked at the buttons on her desk phone. "He's busy on a call right now. Sorry."

Sorry indeed. A thought occurred to me as I headed for the door. "Do you know why Louise left her job here?" I asked.

A solemn look passed over Maggie's face. "I'm sorry to say she passed away."

Good lord! Not another one.

Much to my dismay, Maggie grabbed her ringing phone before I could pursue this subject. Another recently deceased employee was disturbing. It had to fit into my investigation. But how?

Chapter 21

I fretted and stewed as I walked back to my car. Dead agency employees had that effect on me, particularly after my conversation with Peggy and Tiffany last Friday. And from what I had seen, the Ross Agency was a train wreck. No wonder their losses were out-of-control. At some point, I'd need to touch base with their underwriter and discuss this in detail.

My cell phone rang. Peggy.

"Good morning to you," I said, forcing more cheer than I felt.

"Are you on your way here?" she asked.

"I was planning to go directly to Plymouth," I told her, "then stop by the office on my way home if it wasn't too late. Why? What's up?"

"Change your plan," she said. "Stop here first. I think you'll want to pick up your mail."

The ominous tone in Peggy's voice both intrigued and alarmed me. She almost sounded afraid. But that couldn't be. Not my friend Peggy. She wasn't prone to panic.

"Why? What's up with the mail?" I asked.

"I'll tell you when you get here."

I hit the gas pedal hard, anxious to learn what was up.

I abandoned my Mustang in the office parking lot, blocking at least three other cars. No time to search for a real space. I needed to speak with Peggy right away. Besides, I probably wouldn't be long. Nobody would need to get their car out in a hurry. At least I hoped not.

Peggy was in the hallway outside our shared office, fidgeting visibly as she awaited my arrival. "Amy, I'm so glad you're here."

"What's going on?" I asked as I followed her into her office. "What came in the mail?"

"This." She handed me an envelope then plopped into her chair. "Once I saw who it was from, I didn't want to open it without you being here."

That was an odd reaction for Peggy. She was normally down-to-earth and practical in the extreme.

I sat in her visitor's chair and examined the envelope. It was hand-written, in cursive, by a slightly shaky hand. There was no return address, simply the name Tom Foye in the upper left-hand corner. *Holy shit! A missive from a dead man!* This was more than simply upsetting. It was freaking me out.

Peggy watched me intently as I opened the envelope. "I'm sorry if I panicked you," she said. "But getting a letter from the recently departed is pretty creepy. I thought you'd want to know at once, and I didn't want to tell you over the phone."

"Good call," I said as I pulled out a folded paper.

It read: In good conscience, I can no longer bring myself to deal with the Mullins Brothers. I need to get out from under their clutches, but I don't know where to turn. I'm hoping you can be of help. I'll fill you in on all of this when I see you Saturday. Please don't be late. This can't wait. And don't tell anybody you're coming. It was signed simply T. F.

As I pondered this message, I realized something else was in the envelope as well. I reached in to find a business card. And what I saw was disturbing. The card was plain and simple, white with black print. It said: Mullins Brothers Services. Always effective, always discreet. The address was listed as 66 Mountain Road, Sharon, MA.

A bell went off in my head. Pete's neighbor had warned him about Mountain Road. She said he should avoid it. It was haunted. Or evil. Or something equally upsetting. Yikes! And now I learned that the mysterious Mullins brothers lived there! Were they part of whatever alleged evil existed on that road? What was their connection to Tom Foye? Or to my investigation? And why couldn't Tom have lived long enough to let me know what was going on? At this moment, the only thing I knew for sure was that I needed to learn a lot more about both Mountain Road and the Mullins Brothers. And I needed to learn it now.

"Is everything all right?" Peggy asked. "You look as if you've just seen a ghost."

"Or heard from one." I sucked in a large breath and worked at composing myself. "When you're looking for info on the Mullins Brothers, can you please see what you can learn about Mountain Road in Sharon? It seems to have a slightly wonky reputation."

"Sure. Right," she said. She stared at the business card. "Whoever these Mullins Brothers are, they certainly aren't very professional. Either that or they're just plain cheap, not to mention sloppy."

"Why do you say that?" I asked, intrigued by her comment.

"Just look at this card," she said. "It's a mess. There are scribbles on the back. Like the paper they were printed on had been used before."

I examined the back of the card. "These aren't scribbles, Peggy. This is Ogham."

"What's that?" she asked.

"It's an ancient Celtic alphabet. You see it a lot in Ireland, mostly carved on stones."

Peggy took the card from me and examined it again. "So this is like a secret code."

"Sure looks that way," I told her. "And the Mullins Brothers are using it on their business cards. They're communicating something with it. The question is—what? This is alarming."

"So what do we do?"

"We decipher it. Break the code. If anybody can do that, you can. You're good at this sort of thing."

Peggy stared at the back of the card. "I always did love a puzzle," she said. "I'll see what I can do."

That settled for the moment, I continued, "Other than the Mullins brothers, how are you and Tiffany doing with your respective research?"

Peggy shrugged. "We're plugging along. No big break-throughs to report yet. And George is giving Tiffany a hard time. He says she's spending too much time on this and neglecting her other duties. Then he caught her watching the Rhode Island news a while ago and went ballistic. I couldn't even try to explain that she was looking for information on Tom Foye's murder. He wouldn't calm down long enough to listen. I just had to let him rant."

"No surprise there. I think I better get out of here now before he realizes I'm around. I'll deal with him later. And with Mark as well. In the meantime, I've got an appointment in Plymouth this afternoon. Let's plan for you, Tiffany and me to get together tomorrow morning to compare notes and brainstorm. My last scheduled agency appointment is tomorrow afternoon in Hingham. Lord, I hope I'll learn something worthwhile and that can be the end of these visits. In the meantime, let me know if anything comes up." I said a silent prayer that something would indeed come up as I hit the road for Plymouth. There were two agencies remaining in my original plan. If neither of these panned out, I could be back to square one.

Chapter 22

I listened to classic rock music on the way to Plymouth, the Beatles and the Rolling Stones. A taste for this music was one of the best gifts my father ever gave me. It helped me clear my mind and tune out for a while. I needed that today.

A trip to Plymouth, aka America's Home Town, was always a treat. The town had a vibe all its own, quaint and historic without being overly cutesy about it. And the drive along the ocean—past Plymouth Rock and the replica of the Mayflower—was pleasant this time of year. Bright sun, calm blue ocean. And it was too early in the year to be overrun with tourists.

The Michael Morris Agency was on Leyden Street, the location of the Pilgrims' original settlement. For once, I lucked out and found a parking spot nearby. I sat in the car for a few minutes to review the Morris file. They had been with NEC&I for a little more than five years. During that time, we had seen a slow, steady stream of new business with no real issues. Over the past year, though, the quantity of new business had increased considerably, as had the losses. *Coincidence?* I thought not.

The first thing I noticed when I entered the office was the quiet buzz, not unlike being inside a bee hive. There were half a dozen people busy at work—on the phone, clacking away at their computers, speaking with clients—all in muted, professional voices. And everybody was clad in professional business attire. That was something I hadn't seen much of lately. It was a nice change.

A fellow sporting a three-piece blue suit and recently-styled hair approached me. He appeared to be in his mid-thirties, pleasant looking, though not exactly handsome. He had a nice smile. "You must be Ms. Lynch," he greeted me with an overly-firm handshake. Everything about him exuded confidence. Or was it cockiness? Sometimes it was tough to tell the difference.

"It's nice to meet you, Mr. Morris." I returned his smile.

"You're right on time," he said. "Let's go into my office. So we can speak in private." He indicated the way.

I followed.

His office was small, neat and well-appointed. It smelled of freshly-brewed coffee and lemon furniture polish. His computer screen was dark. A neat stack of manila file folders sat on the desk.

Once seated and settled, he favored me with that smile again. "So, what can I do for you today? Apparently there are some recent losses you want to discuss?" He glanced at the file folders on his desk. "Funny, we rarely use paper files these days. Most of our business is done on computer. Claims are somehow different, though."

"Did you have a chance to look those over?" I asked.

"Sure did," he said. "From what I could see, they're all pretty straight-forward. Fairly routine burglaries. Nothing particularly note-worthy about any of them."

I wasn't quite sure what made a burglary routine—or noteworthy. "The issue is more one of overall volume. You've had over twice the expected number of thefts in the last year or so. And always jewelry. Diamonds to be exact."

He studied his fingernails. "Is that so?"

"It is," I said in my stern schoolteacher voice.

He continued, "Do you think the increased numbers could be due to the fact that our business has mushroomed in the last two years? We're growing like crazy these days."

"We actually took that into account," I told him. "According to our actuaries, your numbers are still far higher than expected."

"Hmmm," he said. "I suppose that's good to know."

Good to know? Was that all he had to say? His cavalier attitude didn't sit well with me. "How many companies do you write homeowners insurance with?" I asked.

"We added one about five months ago. That brought us up to four, including NEC&I." Morris beamed at me proudly.

"And how are your loss ratios with the other companies?"

He didn't hesitate to answer. "About the same as with you folks. Although I shouldn't be discussing other companies with you. Why do you ask?"

"Just curious," I said, checking some notes in my file. "You wrote a lot of new homeowners business with us in the past year. Much more than in the prior three or four years."

He beamed again. "Right. As I said, we've been quite fortunate with regard to new business. Our agency is growing even faster than this town is."

Either that or he was moving business around from one company to another to make it all appear to be new—a tactic which would blow up on him at some point.

"In fact," he continued, "I had to increase my staff to handle all the business. Two new full time CSRs this year. Plus one part-timer."

Hmmm. New employees and increased losses? Why was I not surprised? "That must have made a lot of extra work for somebody here. Training new employees can be tough. Not to mention time-consuming."

"Actually not. I simply got lucky."

"How so?"

"All three of the new hires arrived almost fully-trained." He almost smirked as he announced this.

"Oh? Did you lure them away from previous jobs or local competitors?" *Is that why you look so smug about it?*

He shrugged. "They're all fairly new to the business, but whoever trained them did a superlative job. All three of them are licensed and conversant in all types of personal insurance, as well as with the Registry of Motor Vehicles and most of the common insurance agency software out there. They're also superb at customer service. Two of them had some experience. The other appears to be a natural. The clients love them."

That was almost too good to be true. "They sound like gems. Wherever did you find these folks?"

"Through Leo Maguire," he said. "He runs an employment agency in Boston. Specializes in insurance personnel. Extremely good insurance personnel. Sure wish I'd known him ten years ago. It would have saved me a lot of time and effort."

"What's the name of his business?"

"Insurance Personnel, Inc.," he said. "On Broad Street in Boston."

That name rang a bell with me. I had heard it somewhere just a few days ago. Exactly where and from whom was eluding me at the moment. I'd check my notes when I got to the office later. Two of my wayward agents using the same employment agency could be a fluke. After all, how many agencies could there be that specialize in insurance personnel? On the other hand, I never did believe in coincidence.

Time to move on and see what else I might learn from Michael Morris. "How is the workload assigned here?" I asked.

He gave me a quizzical look.

"I mean, who handles the new business, or customer service, or claims? Is there a designated person for each of these tasks?"

He shook his head. "No. We work on a straight alpha split. Each CSR does it all for the clients in her split, almost as if each one is a mini-agency all on its own."

I made a mental note to check the names on the claim files, just in case they were all alphabetical neighbors. That could point a finger at one of his employees. Then I looked out of his office door and took a long, hard look at his staff. All female, not one of them over thirty. "You seem to have a young staff," I said.

"Yes indeed," he beamed. "All young and eager, maybe even hungry. They're excellent at up-selling policies and rounding out accounts. Makes my job a lot easier."

Somehow that didn't surprise me.

"I used to have mostly older employees," he continued. "More mature, experienced. I thought they'd reflect stability, inspire confidence. Boy was I ever wrong."

I decided not to waste time speaking with the CSRs. I probably already had all the information I needed on the Michael Morris Agency. Now I just had to sort it all out and compare it to the data from my other visits. Perhaps I'd review it all with Sam when I walked him tonight. That always seemed to help. Sam didn't say much, but as always he was a wonderful listener. On that note, I jumped into my Mustang and headed for home.

Chapter 23

Sam and I hadn't come to any conclusions the night before, so Peggy, Tiffany and I sat down together in my office the first thing Tuesday morning. We needed to brainstorm. It was Peggy's turn to go first.

"I'll be quick," she said. "And in this case, that's not a good thing."

Tiffany gave her a funny look. "Why not?"

I answered for Peggy. "Because that means she doesn't have much to report."

"Bingo!" Peggy said. "At least not concerning the Mullins Brothers. I'm plugging away at the Ogham on their business card but there's no joy yet. I'm sure I'll figure it out eventually."

"I'm sure you will. I have great faith in you," I told her.

"Thanks. And, despite the fact that these folks have a business card, it's as if they don't actually exist. Or if they do, they're existing under other names. No land-line telephone listing—even looking back over 20 years. Nothing in the Registry of Motor Vehicles database for a Mullins on Mountain Road. The property at 66 Mountain Road is owned by a trust. Nothing comes back on them from Google, Facebook or any other site I could think of. Whoever these guys are, they are masters at keeping a low profile. I even checked Zillow using just their address. I was thinking perhaps I'd take a ride over to Mountain Road some time, to see their house in person."

"Please don't do that," I told her. "At least not alone. I've heard ominous things about that road. Pete's neighbor says it's haunted, and also a dead zone."

Tiffany's eyes grew wide. "Yes, Peggy, please don't go there. If it's a dead zone, you wouldn't be able to call for help."

Realist that she was, Peggy simply continued. "I may not need help, you know, but anyway ... moving right along, I heard back from a few of the police departments I contacted. Two of them are forwarding information to me on a few local burglaries. The rest had nothing to report. Sorry I couldn't come up with anything more helpful."

"Not to worry," I said. "It was a good idea. And the day is still young. Any updates on the hunt for Tom Foye's killer?"

Peggy shook her head. "Nothing new. The police are still looking for the fellow with the funny eye, whatever that means."

"Let's hope they find him soon," I said. "I hate it when there are killers on the loose out there. It takes all the joy out of walking Sam. What about the former CSRs, Tiffany? Did you find anything on what happened to them?"

"This gets a little weird," Tiffany began. She consulted her notes. "Of the ten agencies we investigated, seven of them had a change in personnel due to a death—sometimes it was the employee, sometimes an owner or a member of somebody's family. And some of it you already know. Do you want the specifics?"

"Indeed I do," I said.

"Almeida Agency: the owner's son, who worked there, was killed in a car crash. Harlow Agency: The CSR vanished. Body recently found in a shallow grave. Her throat had been cut. At Zoltov, the prior owner sold the business to take care of his ailing father after his mother died. She was hit by a car while crossing the street. A CSR from the Berkshire Agency drowned when her canoe overturned in a local lake The long-time part-time employee at the Nevins Agency left to take a full-time job after her husband died."

"How did he die?" Peggy asked.

"In a hunting accident. Details on that are pretty sketchy."

"That's five," I said. "Do I dare ask about the other two?"

"The CSR from the Ross agency died in a house fire, which may or may not have been accidental. The official cause of death was smoke inhalation. And the wife of the owner of the Zempke Agency, who worked along with her husband is recently deceased. I don't have the details on that yet."

I sucked in a big breath, then let it out slowly. "There's no way in Hell all of this is coincidental. The universe simply doesn't work that way. It may sound like a leap, but I believe somebody out there is killing CSRs, or people near and dear to them. And each death creates a job opening in one of our agencies."

"Should we report this to the police?" Peggy asked.

I thought this over. "Yes we should, but I'm not sure there's a way to do that. Right, but it's just like with the burglaries, no obvious connection among these incidents yet. We know there is one; we just haven't found it yet."

"This is so awful," Tiffany said. "Who knew the insurance business could be so dangerous?"

I studied my list of agencies being investigated. A few had yet to be mentioned. "What about Foye and Maxwell, Tiffany? Any tragic deaths there?"

She shook her head. "Not that I can find. Patti at Foye was there when Tom took over the business. Similar situation at Maxwell. The CSR was there first."

"And the Morris Agency added staff due to growth," I added. "Nevertheless, we do have a disturbing pattern here."

"There's something else," Tiffany said.

I turned to her. "And that is ...?"

"I compared the dates when the new CSRs started with the dates of the burglaries."

"Good thinking," I told her. "I'm guessing the increase in burglaries began not long after the new employees were in place."

"You've got that right!"

The three of us sat in silence and digested this information. Finally, I said, "Great work, Ladies. You have done yourselves proud. It seems that someone is eliminating agency personnel and replacing them with his, or her, own people. These people proceed to research the agency's files to learn which clients have expensive diamonds and then provide this information to the thief."

"Holy shit," Peggy said. "That's unbelievable."

"Unbelievable and then some," I said, amazed to hear Peggy say shit. In all the years I had known her, that was a first. "So, we've got the middle of the set-up figured out. Now we need to know three things: One—How do these new CSRs manage to infiltrate the agencies? Two—Who is the instigator, the supposed brains of the operation? And three—Who is on the other end, receiving the jewels and converting them into cash?"

A dark cloud passed over Peggy's face. "Is that all? That's a lot of missing information. And here I thought we had made significant progress."

"We have," I said. "And here's what our next step should be. Call all the agents except for Foye and ask how they acquired these new hires. If they used an employment agency, get all the details. OK?"

"Sounds like a plan," Peggy said. "We'll get right on it."

"But wait," Tiffany spoke up. "There's one more thing."

"What's that?" I asked.

"I followed up on the latest diamond theft like you asked. It came from an agency with several recent jewel thefts, though not on our top ten list."

"And?" I asked.

"It sounds sort of petty after all those murders, but I still have to say ... I can't believe how sloppy these people are."

"What do you mean?" Peggy and I both said at once.

"Just look at these appraisals. They're a mess. The margins are full of scribbles, or dirt, or something. Like they all needed to clean their copy machines. Or they were using soiled paper. It's so unprofessional."

"Let me see those," I said.

Tiffany held out the file. As I reached for it, something small fell out of it and onto my desk. And my heart nearly stopped. The Mullins Brothers' business card. *Holy shit! It was all falling into place.* "These aren't scribbles, or doodles or anything like that, Tiffany. And they're definitely not accidental. They're messages. In Ogham."

Peggy gasped.

"And they're showing up on copies of jewelry appraisals. This must be how they're passing the information along to the thief, or thieves. And the Mullins brothers are somehow in the thick of it. I'm not sure how, but they're obviously involved."

"Sounds like progress to me," Peggy said.

"From your lips to God's ears. And just for the record, please consider this proof positive of the value of paper files. As good as our computer system is, we never would have seen these markings there."

Peggy rolled her eyes but had the good sense to bite her tongue.

I reviewed my plans for the day. "I wish I didn't have to go Hingham this afternoon. I'll try to make this visit a quick one. Right about now I think my time would be better spent staying here and continuing to brainstorm with you folks."

Chapter 24

For some unknown reason, there was always traffic on Route 3 heading south from Boston. It was even worse than usual today due to heavy rain. This was particularly annoying, since I felt like I was wasting my time. Odds were I wouldn't learn much of anything new with this final agency visit. I would have preferred to spend the afternoon in the office working with Peggy and Tiffany on our newly-discovered leads. Nevertheless, there I was, inching my way south. My destination, Zempke Insurance, was in Hingham, a lovely little town on the coast.

I smiled and relaxed as I exited the highway. Eleanor Roosevelt once said that Hingham had the most beautiful Main Street in America. I had to agree with her. The road was dotted with colonial era homes—some small and quaint, others stately and elegant—all set back from the road, nestled in finely-manicured lawns and reminiscent of a simpler time. Even in the rain, they looked lovely.

Hingham square was a treat as well. It had charming little shops and restaurants, all locally-owned. Not a single chain store among them. There were store-front businesses and offices as well, Zempke Insurance among them. I parked my Mustang a block up the street, opened my umbrella and forged on, forcing myself to hope for something of interest. The file on this agency was bland to the point of boring. Nothing exceptional, or remarkable in any way. Except for those damn diamond thefts.

The office was small and neat. Also very quiet. A solitary young woman sat at a desk looking bored. She was brunette, slightly overweight, and had crooked teeth. I was pretty sure she wasn't the owner, Kenneth Zempke. She jumped up when I entered. "Good afternoon. Can I help you with something?"

"I'm Amy Lynch from New England Casualty and Indemnity," I told her." I have a 2:00 appointment with Mr. Zempke."

She wrinkled her brow. "Oh, yeah. Right. Sorry, but Kenny's not here today. He called in sick this morning. He has the flu, or some such thing. I meant to call you earlier to reschedule your appointment. Then things got busy. I guess it slipped my mind. My bad. Sorry to drag you all the way here for nothing. Do you want to come back some time next week?"

I gave that idea some thought. "That may not be necessary. Maybe you can help me with the information I need."

"I'll do my best. By the way, I'm Andrea. It's nice to meet you. Have a seat."

I seated myself by Andrea's desk, hoping she'd have something worthwhile to contribute. As long as I was already there, it was worth a shot. "How long have you worked here?"

"A little over three years now."

That was a positive beginning. She may have been there long enough to have something of interest to report. "We're doing a state-wide study of losses in the past year. Burglaries in particular. Is that something you'd have information on?"

Andrea screwed up her face. "Sorry, but I hardly ever handled claims. That was always Mrs. Zempke's job."

Bummer. "Is there any chance I might speak with her?"

"I'm afraid not. Elena, that's Mrs. Zempke, passed away nine or ten months ago."

That was not good news. "I'm sorry to hear that. What happened to her?"

"Heart attack."

That was a relief after my conversation with Peggy and Tiffany this morning. Nothing remotely nefarious about a heart attack.

But Andrea wasn't finished speaking. "During a home invasion," she added. "It was awful. Nearly tore Kenny apart."

It wasn't setting all that well with me either. Had she been scared to death? "Have you been handling the claims since then?"

"No. That was Shannon's job. She was Mrs. Z's replacement."

"Then I guess I'd like to speak with Shannon. Is she in today?"

Andrea shook her head. "She had a baby just last week. She's on maternity leave for the next two months."

And around and around it went. Employees in the claims position at the Zempke Agency had been playing musical chairs. "Who is handling Shannon's claims job while she's out?"

"That'd be Moira. She only just started this past Monday, but she seems to know what she's doing. Wherever she worked before here, somebody trained her well."

I looked around the nearly-deserted office. "And where is Moira now?"

"Gone to the post office." Andrea glanced at the wall clock. "She's been gone a while. Should be back soon. Unless she's lost again."

"What do you mean?"

Andrea sighed. "Well, Moira seems to know a lot about insurance, but she doesn't know her way around Hingham yet. Got herself lost on her way to work two days in a row. I sure hope she finds her way back here. The post office is not that far away."

I hoped so as well. "Were you able to pull the claim files I wanted to discuss with Mr. Zempke?"

"I was. They're on the desk in Kenny's office. He was planning to look them over this morning."

Our conversation ceased as the door opened and a whirlwind of red hair bustled in. My guess was it was Moira.

"Sorry it took me so long, Andrea. There was a long line at the post office. Did I miss anything?" she asked.

I turned to greet her, then my jaw fell open as I gazed into a familiar face. It took me a minute to place where I'd seen her before. Then it hit me. The waitress from Café Begorrah! Now this was a surprising turn of events. Surprising and then some.

Moira gave me a befuddled look.

"This is Amy Lynch from one of our insurance companies," Andrea said to her. "She's here to ask us about some recent claims."

I worked at composing my face, then said, "Moira and I have met before. At an Irish restaurant in Sharon. So this is the new job you told me about the other day. How is it going so far?"

Moira looked everywhere except at me. "Fine, fine," she stammered. "I believe I'm going to like working here." She gave me a small, weak smile. "It's odd that I should run into you here, though. Small world, don't you think?"

My guess was the world was considerably smaller than Moira wanted it to be right about now. I decided to play dumb for a while and let my mind work on fitting the puzzle pieces together. "It's a bit of a hike from Sharon to here. How are you dealing with the commute?"

"Oh, it's not that bad. So far, anyway, I've been taking the back roads. Less traffic, you know. I think it'll be all right. Besides, it's a much better job. I'm glad for the extra money. And maybe I'll end up moving somewhere closer to here. Can't afford to live in Hingham, though. This town is expensive."

In an effort to stop Moira's nervous babbling, I decided to make a graceful exit. "You know, ladies, I think I might as well be on my way. Since neither of you had anything to do with the claims I'm investigating, there's no point in my wasting your time." Besides, I needed some quiet time to mull over Moira's presence here and figure out what it all meant.

"Right, sure," Moira said, visibly relaxing at the thought of my exit. "It was nice to see you again."

I doubted that.

"Do you want me to have Kenny call you when he's feeling better?" Andrea asked. "So you can reschedule your meeting?"

"That may not be necessary. I'll get back to you in a week or so. Enjoy your day."

I hurried back to my Mustang, eager to return to the office and fill Peggy and Tiffany in on Moira's appearance in Hingham. I jumped back onto Route 3 only to find the traffic at a dead stop. The woman on the radio said the heavy rain had made the roads slick and a truck had jack-knifed. It was in the process of being removed.

Rather than becoming annoyed at the situation, I was grateful for some time alone with my thoughts. Maybe I'd come up with something useful.

Since I wasn't driving at the moment, and I didn't see any police nearby,

I grabbed my phone and called Peggy to let her know I probably wouldn't make it to the office before the end of the day. The call went straight to voice mail. I left her a rambling message that I'd had some sort of a breakthrough, but I wasn't quite sure what it meant yet. I'd mull it over tonight and tell her all about it in the morning. Perhaps by then I'd have a better idea about what was going on. And how and why Moira from the Café Begorrah was now working at the Zempke Agency.

Chapter 25

I telephoned Pete the minute I got home—ostensibly to tell him about both Moira and the Mullins Brothers. My main goal was to see how he was doing. I was concerned about him. The break-in and burglary had taken its toll on him.

"Ames, hi. How's it going? I was planning to give you a buzz as soon as the guys are done here."

"Guys?" I asked. "What guys? Is tonight your new poker night or something?"

That got a small laugh out of him. "No. The guys from ADT."

"ADT?"

"Sure," he said. "You know, the home security company. They installed a top-of-the-line system in my office earlier today. Now they're doing the same at the house."

"Good idea. Anything to prevent another break-in."

"Right. Knowing somebody had been in my house made me so angry. I felt like I'd been violated. Not a good feeling."

My heart went out to him. "It's too bad you didn't have the system in place before your mother's ring was stolen."

"That's what I was going to call to tell you. I have some good news to report."

"Oh?"

"The local police just called. They have my mother's ring. Found it when they busted a local jeweler they suspected of being a fence."

"That's wonderful, Pete. How did they know it was your mother's?"

"There was a picture of it on the old appraisal. I gave them a copy of it when I filed the report."

"I'm delighted this worked out so well for you. Now, get that ring into a safe deposit box ASAP," I told him.

"Yes, ma'am," he said. "So tell me, what's up with you? How is your day going?"

I gave him an abbreviated update on how my case was progressing, with special emphasis on the unexpected meeting with Moira.

"The waitress from Begorrah?" he said. "That's one crazy coincidence."

"Or not," I replied.

"What do you mean?"

"I'm not sure yet what I mean. I'll let you know as soon as I figure it out. And, just for the record, there's no such thing as coincidence. You should know that by now."

I could almost hear his eyes rolling.

"Whatever," he said. "Listen, I need to hang up now. The guys are finishing up here. I'll talk with you tomorrow. Maybe by then you'll know what you mean."

Sam had been pacing the kitchen floor while I was speaking with Pete. "Thanks for being patient, buddy," I said to him. "It's your turn now." I grabbed his leash and off we went.

It was a nice evening for a walk—mild enough not to require a heavy coat and not quite dark yet. I loved it when the days started getting longer. Sam and I took the longer version of our evening stroll, and took our time with it as well. I had a lot to tell him about the latest developments, both at work and with Pete. As usual, my canine pal listened with rapt attention.

"It must be one fine story you're telling that dog," a voice from behind me said. I turned around to see my neighbor, Tim O'Malley, with a broad grin on his face and a particularly good-looking dog on a leash.

"Hello, Tim," I said. "I haven't seen you in ages."

"I don't get out so much in the winter anymore, don't you know."

"Is that a new dog? I don't remember seeing him before."

"Right," Tim said. "My poor Jacko passed on in early December. I waited until spring to replace him with this pup. I've had him nearly three weeks now. We're having a fine time getting to know each other."

DEADLY DIAMONDS

Sam gave the pup the usual canine once-over. He was always happy to make a new friend.

"He sure is a beautiful dog," I said, admiring his tight gray-blue curls. "He puts me in mind of a Brillo soap pad. A very cuddly one. What breed is he?"

"He's a Kerry Blue Terrier," Tim said. "They're wonderful dogs, you know. From County Kerry, Ireland. Good working dogs. They were originally bred to hunt small game and birds, or to herd cattle and sheep. And they don't shed."

That was always a plus. What more could a person want in a canine companion? "What's his name?"

Tom smiled. "Liam. Liam Desmond O'Malley. A fine Irish name for a fine Irish dog."

I bent down to let the pup smell my hand. "I'm happy to meet you, Liam Desmond O'Malley. I bet you and Sam will be the best of friends."

"It's getting on time for us to be heading home now, Amy. We'll be seeing you." Tim tipped his hat and led his new pup up the street.

Sam and I continued on, as I worked on connecting the various dots in my case. "A fine Irish name, indeed," I said to Sam." And then it hit me. The dots began falling into place. And they were all Kelly green.

Chapter 26

I sat in my office Wednesday morning, eager to fill Peggy and Tiffany in on the Kerry blue terrier with the fine Irish name and what he had helped me to realize. While waiting, I searched online for anything new on Tom Foye's murder. No luck. What had been big news a few days ago had become old news overnight, much to my dismay. It was time to put that issue aside for the moment and work with what information we had.

Peggy arrived with a bounce in her step and a big silly grin on her face. "Good morning to you."

"You're looking rather pleased with yourself," I said. "I'm guessing that means you've come up with something of interest."

"You better believe it," she replied. "Do you want to hear it now or shall we wait for Tiffany?"

Before I could make that decision, Tiffany breezed in the door, slightly out of breath. "Sorry. I got held up. George summoned me to his office and demanded a full accounting of my time over the last few days. He's pretty unhappy with me lately. And he has apparently already forgotten that I actually went to him with a question the other day. I honestly don't know how to please that man."

"Don't worry about it," I told her. "I have a meeting with him and Mark later this morning. It's well past time to get them up-to-date on our progress. If I can make George feel more involved, maybe he'll lighten up on you. And who knows? Maybe he'll have something useful to contribute." *Or not.*

"So how'd you get away from him?" Peggy asked.

"I got lucky. His phone rang just as I began to answer him. It must have been an important call, because he told me, and I quote 'I'm not done with you yet. We'll finish this later.' Later works fine for me." She plopped into a chair. "So what's happening?"

"Peggy has something of interest to tell us," I said, turning to my assistant. "I'm guessing she's made some progress. Take it away Peg."

Peggy beamed. "Progress, and then some. I have decoded the message on the Mullins brothers' business card."

"Wow. That was fast." I said. "I'm impressed."

"I was intrigued. I got on it right away. Even brought it home with me. I translated the Ogham quickly enough. There was no real challenge there once I got the hang of it. But what I came up with wasn't making any sense at first."

"Why not?" Tiffany asked.

"Because it was in Gaelic."

My first reaction was "Good grief!" After a moment's thought, I realized that the message being in Gaelic made perfect sense. "Were you able to translate the Gaelic?"

Peggy hesitated, then replied, "Eventually. That took a while. It's a tricky language. I would have called you when I finally worked it out, but that was around 3:00 this morning."

"Good grief, Peggy, did you get any sleep?"

She shook her head. "Not much. I was so disturbed by what the message says there was no way I could sleep."

I was almost afraid to hear the rest. "So what does it say?"

"You're not going to like this," Peggy said. "Or maybe you won't even believe it. It sure freaked me out. I mean, this simply cannot be real."

I was on the verge of impatience. "What? Tell us."

Peggy sucked in a breath and let it out slowly. "It says 'Death or theft upon request. Your wish is our command. No job too large or too small.'"

Tiffany's mouth fell open. I choked on my coffee.

"Holy Toledo!" Tiffany said. "That's incredible. And pretty darn scary. No wonder you couldn't sleep."

I mulled the message over as I mopped up a puddle of coffee on my desk with shaky hands. "You're right. This is hugely disturbing. It does, however, provide a lot of food for thought. It suggests that vacancies at these agencies are the work of the Mullins brothers."

"That's a hell of a way to create job openings," Peggy said.

I digested the information. "Agreed. It's unconscionable."

Tiffany sat up straight. "And here's where my research from yesterday comes in. About filling those vacancies."

Peggy and I gave her our full attention.

"I spoke with the agents we discussed. They all used the same employment agency for their most recent hires. It's in Boston."

"Let me guess," I said, searching my brain for the name I'd heard recently. "Insurance Personnel, Inc.? On Broad Street?"

"Right," Tiffany said, then added, "Clever name, don't you think?"

"Clever scheme," I added. "Ruthless, deadly, and, sadly, quite effective. The question now is: how do we proceed from here?"

"And remain alive, you mean?" Tiffany asked.

I nodded. "That would be the goal."

"We need to take this to the police," Peggy said. "And let them handle it."

"I don't think we can do that, Peg. At least not yet," I told her.

"But why?" she asked.

"First of all, it's a question of jurisdiction," I said. "You should know that."

Peggy wrinkled her brow. "You're right. I don't think so well on no sleep. But now that you bring it up, you're right. How would we ever know which police to contact? These agencies are all over the state."

"I believe that would be the job of the state police," I said. "Except I'm not sure we have enough evidence to go to them yet. As good as our information is, a lot of it is conjecture. We'll need to come up with something more concrete in the way of proof before involving them. We need something that definitely ties it all together. And I think we're almost there."

"Do you mean that everything we know about the CSRs isn't enough?" Tiffany asked.

"Not quite, but we have added a few pieces to the puzzle. It fits in nicely with the Ogham writing. And it puts us one step closer to the answer," I said. "And it works well with something I realized last night."

"What's that?" Peggy asked.

I proceeded to give them the low-down on the Kerry Blue Terrier with the fine Irish name. "And that's when it occurred to me that the CSRs in the agencies I had visited all had fine Irish names as well." I referred to the notes I had scribbled last night. "There's Sheila, Maureen, Kate, Deirdre, Alana, Maggie and, of course, the ever-popular Moira. The bottom line is that pretty much everybody involved appears to be Irish. That can't be merely a coincidence."

I then told them about Moira from Café Begorrah and her sudden appearance at Zempke Insurance in Hingham—and how she fit into the same profile as the CSRs in the other agencies. "Now all we need to learn is who is behind this dreadful scheme, as well as how the diamonds are being converted into cash. You've done excellent work on this, Ladies. Nice going. The missing link is out there somewhere. And I think we'll find it before long."

Tiffany listened, her eyes wide. "Wow, Amy. You're right. I can't believe I didn't see that. It looks like I still have a lot to learn."

"Don't beat yourself up, Tiff," I said. "You're doing just fine."

After finishing up with Peggy and Tiffany, I headed up to Executive Heaven to meet with Mark and George. I had been putting that off for several days. Now I was looking forward to it. It was good to have something positive to report.

"Amy, hi, come on in," Mark said.

George turned in his seat and smirked up at me. "Hello, Hotshot. Long time no see. How have you been? How's life on the road?"

"Hello, George. Did you miss me?" I plopped into the chair next to him and flashed him what I meant to be my sweetest smile. From the look on his face, apparently it wasn't working.

Mark gave me a disapproving look. "How is the case going, Amy?"

I gave them a detailed accounting of everything Peggy, Tiffany and I had learned so far.

George shook his head.

"What's up, George?" Mark asked. "You look as if you're not convinced that Amy's on the right track."

I bit my tongue, curious to learn what he thought.

"I'm not convinced of anything," George said. "Based on my statistical research, I'm beginning to wonder if this entire situation is nothing but a colossal fluke. Something that, against all odds, simply happened by random chance. A one in a million occurrence."

Even though you're the one who brought these thefts to our attention in the first place? Give me a break. "I believe we disagree on that point," I told him.

Mark frowned. "It would be a rather large fluke, not to mention an expensive one."

"I'd like to continue with my investigation for a while," I said. "I believe it will be worth the effort."

Mark nodded. "Sorry, George. I have to agree with Amy on this one."

George sighed loudly. "Whatever you want. In that case, please forward the particulars of your information to me, Amy. I'll check it against the data I've collected and see what develops."

I wasn't quite sure what that meant, so simply said, "Sure, George. No problem. And can you please forward me your current results as well?"

Marked watched our exchange with a bemused look on his face.

George scowled. "That'll have to wait a day or two. It's not quite ready yet. I have been putting significant time into covering for Tiffany while she has been off having coffee and gossiping. I hope that phase of this investigation will end shortly."

"I believe it will. And you both need to know that Tiffany's contribution has been invaluable. The girl has good instincts. She's wonderful with people, gets them talking. She manages to sift through her information and see patterns. Very helpful patterns. We're lucky to have her on our side."

"That's good to know," Mark said.

George gave me a dirty look.

"So how much more time do you need to put this mess to bed?" Mark asked.

"Just give me a couple of days to fill in the few remaining blanks. We still have some questions to work out. It shouldn't take long."

George glared at me.

Mark nodded. "Good luck."

"Thanks." I smiled at them both and hoped the luck of the Irish would rain down on me. And fast.

Chapter 27

Back in my own office, I looked up the number for Insurance Personnel, Inc. and placed the call. The phone rang seven times before being answered.

"Insurance Personnel," a male voice growled. "You can either hold or call back later. I'm on another call right now."

It sounded like this was a one-person operation—which seemed to consist of a not-so-very-pleasant person and an office system that didn't have proper voice mail. Somehow I had expected something more professional from a business on Broad Street in Boston.

I chose to wait. It gave me a chance to check through the ever-growing pile of unread mail on my desk, not to mention an abundance of unread emails. As I opened the fourth or fifth envelope, I heard, "Yeah. Hi. Thanks for holding." He didn't sound thankful.

"Hello. My name is Meghan O'Reilly," I lied. "I just moved to Boston from Hartford, Connecticut and I need a job. I've had loads of experience in insurance. I worked as a CSR in Hartford for nearly fifteen years. What do ...?"

"You can stop right there, Lady," he spat into the phone. "Sorry, but I won't be able to help you."

He didn't sound very sorry to me. "But why is that?" I asked.

"Supply and demand," he said, with more than a trace of impatience in his voice. "I've got more candidates available at the moment than I have openings for them to fill. Looks like lots of insurance agencies simply aren't hiring right now. At least not through me. You'll have to look somewhere else."

This time he didn't even say he was sorry. "Oh dear!" I said. "Are you sure? Couldn't you please just meet with me? Or take my name and contact information in case jobs open up sometime soon?" I did my best to sound a little desperate. It could be helpful to see how far I could push this guy, and what—if anything—he'd have to say. "Like I said, I'm new to Boston. I don't know where else to look for a job. And I need to find one right away. I've nearly run through my savings simply moving here and setting myself up in an apartment. And my rent is due in less than a week. Could you please at least just put me on your list?"

"Sorry, Lady. No can do." And he disconnected the call without even wishing me better luck elsewhere. *What was up with that?* I was working through all possible reasons for an insurance personnel business to treat prospective insurance personnel like that when Peggy popped into my office and put a package on my desk. It was a cardboard box around twelve inches on all sides, wrapped in brown paper and twine, with my name and office address block printed in red magic marker.

"This just arrived for you," Peggy announced. "UPS. It's marked personal and confidential. And urgent."

"And there's no return address," I added. "That's odd." I picked up the package, shook it, turned it upside-down. Not very heavy. And nothing was written on it beside what Peggy had already read.

"Aren't you going to open it?" Peggy asked.

I took in a deep breath, then let it out slowly. "I guess it's all right to. After all, it's not heavy enough to be a bomb. And it isn't ticking." I grabbed a pair of scissors from my desk drawer and cut the twine, then the paper. There was a flimsy cardboard box inside, taped closed. I removed the tape from all four sides, lifted the cover and pulled out a wad of tissue paper wrapped around something soft. I began to remove the tissue paper. Then my heart stopped.

"Oh my God!" Peggy shouted as I unwrapped a stuffed animal—a dog—which looked remarkably like my Sam. Except that this one had a noose around its neck.

Unable even to scream, I dropped the stuffed dog onto the floor and grabbed the edges of my desk for support.

Peggy jumped into action. "Amy, are you all right? This is awful! Please sit down. Put your head between your legs. And stay that way for a couple of minutes."

Ignoring her advice, I flopped back into my chair and took several yoga breaths in a pathetic attempt to slow down my racing heart.

Peggy picked the dog up off the floor, holding it like it might possibly be poisoned, and placed it on my desk. "This is frightening. Who would do such a thing?" she asked. "And why?"

Still unable to speak, I sat there and stared at Sam's unfortunate doppelganger. The noose around its neck was terrifying. It was disturbing enough that somebody felt the need to threaten me. That happens once in a while in my business. But leave my Sam alone. He did nothing to deserve this.

"I'm going to call the police," Peggy said. "Somebody out there is threatening you, and the cops need to do something about it. Now."

"No. Not yet!" I banged my hand on the desk, as I finally found my voice. "Give me a few moments to pull myself together. To think this through. To figure out what I've got here. And what I'm still missing. Whatever you do, don't touch anything, particularly the noose. There should be fingerprints on the rope." I continued breathing slowly and looking at the poor stuffed dog in disbelief.

Peggy waited silently, watching me as if she expected me to faint, or cry.

I chose not to do either. I sucked in a breath and did my best to remain calm. "We can't let this frighten us," I said. "If we do, then whoever sent it has already won."

"So what do we do?" she asked.

"We get angry," I told her. "We get rip-shit furious angry. Nobody's going to treat me like this and get away with it. And nobody's going to get away with threatening my Sam. We use our anger as a weapon against whoever did this. We use it to find the bastard, then give him what he deserves."

The look in Peggy's eyes suggested she wasn't convinced about the wisdom of this approach. "Do you want me to call the police now?" she asked. "Maybe they'll know what we've got, And what we're still missing. That is their job, right?"

I struggled to pull myself together. "Yes, please do." I stared down at my shaky hands. "I don't think I can manage a phone at the moment. And also try to reach Pete." As soon as Peggy left the room to place the calls, I put my head into my hands and sobbed.

I managed to pull myself together just before Peggy re-appeared at my door. "I've got Detective Donnelly on the phone for you." She placed a glass of water on my desk. "Here, drink this first. It'll help to calm you down."

"Thanks." I did as instructed, then grabbed the phone. "Hello, Detective."

"Hello, Ms. Lynch. Your associate informs me that you've had a rather upsetting incident. Are you all right?"

I almost thought I heard a note of concern in his voice. "I'm fine," I lied. "But thanks for asking. Did Peggy give you the particulars?"

"She did," he replied. "This is serious business. We need to respond to this threat immediately."

"And how do we do that?" I asked.

"We begin by sending somebody over to your office to check for evidence. Our best hope is to get some fingerprints. The outside wrapping is a lost cause. Too many people have handled that by now."

"What about the twine?"

"That's a possibility. But also rather challenging. It could have too many prints to be of any use to us. The cardboard box inside is a different story, as are the tape, the tissue paper and the stuffed dog. Let's cross our fingers that we find some usable prints on at least one of those items. We take it very seriously when a citizen receives such an obvious threat. We'll do everything we can to discover who did this to you."

"Thanks, Detective. I appreciate that."

"Just doing my job," he replied, then added. "You know, I have somewhat of a personal interest here. You and I got to know each other when we dealt with that death on Chadwick Street. We worked rather well together. I respect your abilities. I wouldn't want to see anything bad happen you."

I breathed an enormous sigh of relief. At least I was in good hands. "Do I need to be here when the crime scene folks arrive?"

"Somebody does," he said. "It doesn't have to be you."

"Good. Because I need to get home and make sure my dog is all right. What if somebody already got to him?"

"Let's take this one step at a time," Donnelly said. "Under no circumstances should you go home alone. It may not be safe. I'm sure this has been very upsetting for you. but you can't be taking any chances."

He was right. "How about if I have somebody walk with me?" I asked. "My apartment is only a few blocks from the office."

"I guess that would be all right, though I'd rather you get a ride there. It might not be a good idea to be out on the street, even if there is someone with you. Go home. Check on the dog. Lock your door and try to relax. But whatever you do, do not answer your door or let anybody in. I'll send an officer over shortly to take a statement from you."

I was getting a mixed message here. "How will I know it's an officer at the door and not somebody trying to harm me?"

"Ask her name."

"Which is?"

"Officer Lilian Davies. Then plan on coming to my office tomorrow morning—let's say around 10:00—and we'll discuss this in greater detail."

"Sounds good," I told him. "I'll see you then."

I had barely disconnected from Detective Donnelly when my cell phone rang. Pete.

"Good Lord, Ames," he said, "Peggy told me what happened. Stay right where you are. I'll be there shortly."

"I'm just about to head home," I told him. "I need to make sure Sam's OK."

"Don't you dare go anywhere alone. That may not be safe. I'm almost to your office. Wait for me."

"What if I have Peggy drive me?"

"Yeah. That's good. And I'll get there as fast as I can."

Chapter 28

Pete was right, of course. So was Detective Donnelly. I was in no shape to go home alone. I was worried about who might follow me there, or what, or whom, might await me. That realization didn't make it any easier to remain in my office waiting for Peggy to get off the phone. I paced around the room, alternately checking the time and watching out my one small window for any stranger who might be lurking there. I concentrated on my growing anger; that helped to stave off the tears.

On my third or fourth tour around the perimeter of the room, Peggy burst in. "Sorry about the wait. Detective Donnelly had a few instructions for me. Grab your things and let's go."

I let out the breath I didn't realize I'd been holding and did as instructed.

We drove the two blocks to Otis Street and pulled up on the street in front of my apartment. Peggy started to exit the car.

"You know you can't park here, right?" I said.

Peggy nodded. "And yet I did. I'm going to escort you upstairs and check the apartment. Just to be sure. Besides, I'd gladly pay a fine to ensure your safety."

"You are a true friend." I attempted to smile at her. My nerves had other ideas.

We ran up the stairs to my third-floor apartment. Peggy unlocked the door for me. My shaking hands weren't quite up to the task. The door flung open and there was Sam, safe and sound, and wagging his entire body, visibly thrilled to see the two of us at an unexpected time of day. I nearly collapsed with relief as I bent over to greet my dog.

Sam and Peggy and I had a joyous group hug then made our way to the couch. Sam was loving the attention, happily unaware of its source.

Peggy had no sooner left than Pete arrived at my door. I let him in, pretty sure Detective Donnelly's mandate didn't apply to my boyfriend. I greeted him with a big bear hug, then bolted the door.

"I'm so glad you're here, Pete," I told him. "You have no idea how scared I was. But how did you get here so fast?"

"Dumb luck," he said. "I was downtown, filing some paperwork at the court house. Crazy coincidence, huh?"

"There's no such thing as coincidence. That was karma, pure and simple."

I snuggled up between Pete and Sam and began to relax. "I wonder if he needs to go out," I said to Pete.

"He'll be all right for a while. I'll take him for a walk when the police officer comes to take your statement." He rose from the couch and headed toward the kitchen. "I'll be right back." And so he was, with two glasses and a nearly-full bottle of single malt scotch. "This will help you to relax."

It did. We sat in comfortable silence for a while, sipping scotch and pulling ourselves together. After a while, Pete asked, "Are you feeling better now, Ames? Beginning to calm down now that you know Sam is safe?"

I nodded.

"Because," he continued, "I don't know what I'd do if I lost you. You are my world."

This conversation was beginning to make me uncomfortable.

He took my hand and read my mind. "There are a lot of things you and I need to discuss at another time. Right now, I think we should concentrate on dealing with the police."

As if on cue, we heard a knock at my door.

"Who's there?" I asked.

"Police. Officer Lilian Davies. I'm here to take your statement."

I rose to let the woman in.

"This is my cue to leave," Pete said, as he attached Sam's leash to his collar. Sam and I will be back in a while."

He and Sam walked out the door. Officer Davies walked in.

My interview with Davies went well enough. No real surprises. After she left, I did some serious thinking. By the time Pete and Sam returned, I had come to a few conclusions and made a few decisions. Then my phone rang. Detective Donnelly. "I was just thinking about calling you," I said.

"And why was that?"

"About tomorrow. Would it be all right if I came later? Noon would be good."

"Why the change in plans?" he asked.

"Something has come up. If what I'm thinking is in fact so, then I may just have a lot more to tell you when we do meet."

He chuckled. "I have no idea what you're talking about, but I'll trust your instincts. From what I've seen before, they're usually right on target. How about noon?"

"That'd be perfect. Is it all right if my boyfriend joins us?"

"Sure no problem."

"Thanks. But you called me just now, didn't you? What's up?"

"We got a match on some prints we took off your package."

That was good news. At least I thought it was. "So we're talking about somebody who is in your system. Somebody who has been in trouble before?"

"Right." Donnelly sighed loudly. "The odd thing is we hadn't heard from this guy in ages. At least ten years, maybe more. It was as if he'd dropped off the face of the earth."

"Or decided to go straight," I suggested.

"No. Not this guy. He was always one bad dude."

"What's his name?"

"Michael Mullins."

I dropped the phone onto the floor.

Chapter 29

I was not at my best Thursday morning. I had barely slept—for a number of reasons. Being threatened by one of the Mullins brothers was frightening. Since Peggy's translation of the ogham on their business card, I knew exactly what they were capable of doing. And it wasn't pretty. I was glad that Pete was with me. At least I felt safe—for the moment, anyway.

Pete and I had sat up most of the night talking things through. We arrived at a pretty good idea of what the Mullins brothers and their cohorts were up to. There was only one more piece to fit into the puzzle. That was my mission this morning.

Pete came with me into Boston. He dropped me at the door of 80 Broad Street, planning to find a place to park, then wait in the car while I took care of business. We also devised a back-up plan, just in case Plan A didn't work. I placed a call to his cell phone, then dropped my phone into my jacket pocket. That way, he could listen to what was happening. And if I needed to be rescued, he'd be there in a flash. We agreed on a secret code word to let him know.

A cheesy, hand-written cardboard sign on a door notified me that Insurance Personnel, Inc. was on the ground floor. It appeared ill-lit and gloomy. The glass in the door was streaked and covered with fingerprints. Nothing professional-looking about it. I girded my loins and marched in to meet Leo Maguire.

The office was small and sparsely furnished. There was a single metal file cabinet, an oversized wooden desk with a computer and telephone on it and very little else. An overweight gray-haired man in an ugly tweed suit sat behind the desk with his back to me. I assumed he was Leo. He was barking into the phone. Apparently somebody had annoyed him royally. I cleared my throat to make sure he was aware of my presence. He held up his left index finger and shouted, "Yeah. Hold on. I'll be with you shortly," then continued his angry conversation. I tried to tune in, hoping to learn what he was discussing. No such luck. I began to pace back and forth in the front of the room rehearsing the cover story Pete and I had concocted. My heels clicked on the tile floor. Not very subtle of me, but it did the trick. My angry friend muttered into the phone, "Gotta go now. Somebody's here. I'll get back to you later."

He spun his chair around to face me. I stopped dead in my tracks.

Holy shit! It was the man from Café Begorrah. The one who always sat at a corner table working on his laptop and snarling at the waitress. Fancy meeting him here, although I wasn't surprised. This merely confirmed my ever-growing suspicions. The good news was that he didn't appear to recognize me, so the plan Pete and I had cooked up might just work. I clenched my fists in my pockets to steady my nerves, pasted a smile on my face and said, "Hello. My name is Eileen O'Rourke. I'm looking for a job. My husband thought my best chance to find something worthwhile, with a good salary and benefits, would be in downtown Boston. I'm hoping you'll be able to help me."

He started to say something. I jumped back in fast before he had the chance. "I've got plenty of experience in personal insurance. Worked as a CSR in Dorchester until the twins were born. They're in kindergarten now. So I'll need to work mother's hours. Or perhaps work from home at least part of the time. Most businesses are happy to do that nowadays, aren't they? I sure hope so, because we need the money badly. With two kids to feed and clothe, we can't make it on Pete's salary alone. And he refuses to take a second job. He says it's time for me to do my part. As if cooking and cleaning and taking care of two little kids wasn't work. But he just doesn't see it that way. And the bills have been piling up. Pete's parking the car right now. He'll be in here in a minute." I took a breath and prayed that

Pete was getting my message. "I think he wants to be sure you give me a fair shot at the best job you've got available. You know how husbands can be, right?"

"I can't help you, Lady," he growled. "I've got no openings to fill at the moment. Sorry."

That was the same thing he had told my alter ego Meghan O'Reilly over the phone. And exactly what I had expected to hear today. I wrung my hands in mock-agitation. "Oh dear. That is a problem. Could you please at least take my information? Let me fill out a form or something? In case something turns up sometime soon. That way, my husband would know I was trying to find a job. Then maybe he'd get off my case for a while. I'd sure appreciate it. Please. This is important to me. Pete has a bad temper. And he insists I have to get back to work as soon as possible."

Mr. Personality shook his head. "Like I said, there's nothing I can do for you. Let's not waste each other's time."

"But my husband will be here in a minute. Can you at least talk to him? And let him know why you can't find me a job?" *Where the hell are you, Pete? I'm running out of mindless drivel and could use a little help here.*

As if in answer to my plea, Pete came through the door. "How's it going, Eileen? Does this dude have a good job for you?" He held his hand out and said, "Hi. I'm Peter O'Rourke. Detective O'Rourke, that is. Boston Police. Pleased to meet you."

Leo Maguire, aka "this dude," sputtered as he reached out to shake Pete's hand. "I'm sorry to say there's nothing I can do for you. Like I was just telling your wife, I've got no openings at the moment."

Pete slammed his fist on the counter. "That is definitely not what I wanted to hear. Are you telling me that I took the morning off and drove my wife downtown all for nothing? What the hell kind of employment agency is this anyway? How do you stay in business if you've got no jobs to fill? I've got to tell you, Mr. Maguire, this is a disappointment, a very big disappointment." He stood there and glared at the man.

Maguire barely reacted to Pete's rant. "Sorry, Pal. Nothing I can do. Good luck to you both. Then he turned his back on us and returned to his desk.

Pete took hold of my elbow. "Come on, Eileen. Let's get out of here. Any job this creep had would probably suck anyway."

I had all I could do to contain myself until we were out of earshot. Then I burst out laughing. "Good God, Pete. Did you have to lay it on that thick?"

Pete laughed as well. "What can I say? Once I got started, I couldn't help myself. And, just for the record, you were laying it on pretty thick yourself before I got there." He laughed again, then said, "I can't believe that was the guy from Café Begorrah, but there's no mistaking that angry face. You must have flipped when you saw him."

"Not really," I replied. "I knew there had to be some sort of connection between the restaurant and this employment agency. It's all falling into place now. It's a surprisingly clever set-up, in an evil sort of way. I'll be interested to see what Detective Donnelly thinks of it."

"Let's bear in mind that this isn't the sole purpose for our visit with the detective," he said. "We need to catch the creep who's threatening you and Sam."

"I know. But it's all interconnected. And as long as we're there we might as well run everything by him. I'm hoping he can do something to help here, or at least point us in the right direction."

Pete looked skeptical. "From your lips to God's ear," he said. "Let's go."

Chapter 30

An hour later, we were in Detective Donnelly's office discussing Michael Mullins' not-so-subtle threat against me. "I assume you want to press charges," the detective said.

"Absolutely," I told him. "Let's nail the sucker."

"That may not be as easy as you think." He frowned. "And I am truly sorry about that."

"But why?" I asked. "What's not easy about this? We know he mailed the package to me. We've got the prints to prove it."

"For one thing, he can say it was just a joke," Donnelly replied.

"That's correct, Amy," Pete added. "It won't be easy to prove actual malicious intent."

They were right, of course, but I didn't care. "Let's at least give it a try."

Donnelly sighed. "If you insist. But first we're going to have to find him. The guy's been in the wind for years."

"Piece of cake," I told him. "Try 66 Mountain Road in Sharon. That's the address listed on his business card."

"Why am I not surprised that you know this when we don't?" Donnelly asked. "I have always suspected you're some sort of witch."

That made me laugh. "What can I say? I have my ways."

The detective made a few notes. "All right. If you're sure you want to go through with this, I'll contact the Sharon Police to give us a hand. And please, work with them. Don't try to handle things on your own. From what I saw of his record, Michael Mullins is a dangerous character. I'd hate to see anything unfortunate happen to you."

"Then we'll simply have to make sure that nothing bad does happen," I said, with considerably more bravado than I felt. "There's no way I'm going to let this son of a bitch scare me off."

Pete took my hand. "Are you sure, Ames? Absolutely sure? You could be putting yourself in danger."

"Not to worry, Pete," I said. "What I am sure about is that both you and Detective Donnelly will take good care of me. So let's get on with it."

Donnelly gave me a mock salute. "Yes, Ma'am."

That settled, I steeled myself to broach the next subject. "As long as we're here, Detective, there is something else, something related, that I'd like to discuss with you. While I know this is outside of your jurisdiction, I hope that you can help me sort it out, maybe point me in the right direction."

He checked his watch. "I have a few minutes to spare. I guess it can't hurt to listen."

Pete and I proceeded to give him the low-down on my case, in all its painfully bizarre details.

Donnelly listened politely, even took some notes. "That's quite a story, Ms. Lynch. I'll give you that."

"It's more than a story," I replied. "I'm convinced that I'm right. I just don't quite know how to proceed."

"OK. Let's talk it through," he said. "Look at it objectively. I'll play the devil's advocate for you."

"That's all we can ask," Pete said.

Donnelly glanced at the notes he had taken. "If I understand you correctly, what you're telling me is that a group of Irish thugs has concocted this hugely complex plan to steal high-valued jewelry."

"Diamonds," I said. Then I bit my tongue. *Shut up, Amy*, I reminded myself. *You're here to enlist Donnelly's help, not to piss him off by correcting him.*

"Yeah, right. What exactly is it that makes you believe these thugs are Irish?"

That was easy. "Because the restaurant's Irish. And there's a framed picture of Whitey Bulger on the wall."

"That is something you don't see all that often, nor would you want to," he said. "But what does it truly mean?"

"And there are never any customers in the restaurant except for me and Pete. I'm sure it only exists to launder money."

"Either that or the food's no good," Donnelly said.

Pete replied to that, "As a matter of fact, the food is excellent. And from what I've seen of the Café Begorrah, I feel that Amy may be correct about its purpose."

Donnelly frowned. "Even if that were true, don't you think this whole scenario is a little far-fetched? I mean, really, you're telling me that these thugs are killing insurance agents simply so they can replace them with their own people?"

"They're hiring the Mullins brothers to do the actual killing," I reminded him.

Donnelly stared out the window. "So you say. But there's no guarantee the insurance agencies in question will go to that downtown personnel agency. They could find new employees any number of places."

"You're right," I said. "And we've no way of knowing how often this may have happened. But we do know that many of the agents we've investigated have gone to Insurance Personnel, Inc., an employment agency that doesn't seem to be interested in working with walk-in, or phone-in, job seekers. And Insurance Personnel, Inc. and Café Begorrah are run by the same person. We've proved that."

Pete chimed in, "All the 'new' customer service reps are either Irish or married to an Irishman. That's a fact."

"So it seems," Donnelly said. "But you can't prove that the deaths connected to these businesses are related to each other in any way. Or even that they're actually murder. Some could very well have been accidents."

"And therein lies the problem," Pete said. "The pattern is there. Every time. A CSR dies in some slightly odd way, a young Irish woman replaces her and the office suffers a rash of jewelry thefts."

"And you say these burglaries are perpetrated by the Mullins brothers?"

"Yes," I told him, "based on information the new CSRs are obtaining in customer files. And sometimes they sell the coverage themselves, as a rider to an existing policy. By the time the Mullins brothers receive the information, they know exactly which diamonds are where, and how much they're worth."

Donnelly didn't appear convinced. "And you're saying that they forward this information to the Mullins brothers, using some sort of a code in secret Irish hieroglyphics."

I nodded. "Right. It's called Ogham. It's an ancient Celtic alphabet."

"And all the CSRs know this code. As do the Mullins brothers?"

"Yes," I said. "Just look at what it says on their business card. 'Death or theft upon request. Your wish is our command. No job too large or too small.'"

"So you say," Donnelly replied. "It looks more like chicken scratch to me. It's all just a bit too fantastical. If I didn't know you better, Ms. Lynch, I might find myself wondering what you've been smoking."

There was no polite way for me to respond to that.

"You do have to admit that it all fits together nicely," Pete said.

"Perhaps too nicely," Donnelly replied. "And like I said, you have no real proof."

"Right," Pete agreed. "At least not yet."

Donnelly screwed his face up, as if in deep thought. "And this is still mainly nothing but supposition and conjecture. A little light on actual facts."

"What about the fact that the fellow from Bogorrah just happens to run the personnel agency in Boston? Or the fact that somebody just threatened me?" I asked. "Don't these count for something?"

"Something, sure," Donnelly replied. "But it's not enough. There's nothing obvious that ties it all together."

I had to concede on that point. "We know," I said. "The fact that this rash of diamond thefts is spread at random throughout the state doesn't help us either. No individual police department would zero in on it. At least not for a long time. Only an insurance company would see the bigger picture. You have to admit that is clever."

"If it's true," Donnelly conceded. "But that would mean that we're dealing with multiple jurisdictions here."

"My point exactly," I said. "How does law enforcement even begin to investigate a scheme like this? That's why we came to you, so you can point us in the right direction. Is this something for the FBI?"

"Technically, yes. But it is a remote possibility since the crimes in question are confined to Massachusetts," the detective responded.

"I'm assuming jurisdiction would lie with the state Police," Pete said.

Donnelly nodded. "You'd be right, if they'd bother to become involved. Based on what you've given me so far, I honestly can't see that happening."

I wasn't ready to give up yet. "Please, think, detective. There has to be something we can do to expose these people."

He stared at the ceiling for a moment. "OK. Here's what I can do for you. There's a guy at the state police barracks in Foxboro. That's their closest location to Sharon. He owes me a favor. Let me give him a call and see if he'll at least hear you out. Maybe he'll come up with something we haven't thought of."

"Would you be willing to do that for us?" Pete asked.

"I shouldn't tell you this," Donnelly replied, "but I've developed a soft spot for Ms. Lynch. I'll give my friend a call. His name is Nathan Holt."

"Detective, I could kiss you," I said.

He almost smiled. "It'd probably be better if you didn't. I'll let you know what Nate says."

Chapter 31

Detective Donnelly called my office late that afternoon. "Nate has agreed to sit down with you," he said. "Based on what I told him, he's pretty skeptical, but at least he's willing to listen. Be there at 9:00 tomorrow morning. I wish you luck."

"That's wonderful news," I told him. "Thanks, Detective. I owe you one."

I called Pete to let him know, then packed a bag. Sam and I jumped into my Mustang and headed to Massapoag Junction. If I needed to be in Foxboro at 9:00 in the morning, it made sense to be close by. It'd be good for Sam as well. He loved running freely in Pete's fenced-in yard and harassing the local ducks.

Pete had dinner waiting for us when we arrived—spaghetti and meatballs, one of his best culinary achievements. Sam enjoyed the meatballs. Pasta wasn't one of his favorites. We watched an old movie, walked Sam and made it an early night. Better to be fresh and well-rested in the morning. Not to mention convincing.

Pete and I took separate cars to the state police barracks in Foxboro. He needed to get to his new office by late morning to meet with a client. I had to work as well, but first needed to head back to Pete's house, pick up Sam and drop him at my apartment before going to the office. The morning traffic on Route 1 was annoying, though not as bad as Boston rush hour. We met in the state police parking lot, where I joined Pete in his car since we had some time to kill.

"Why do they call this place a barracks instead of a station?" I asked. "The name makes it sound like troopers are living there."

"They used to," he told me. "Back in the early days, a trooper would be assigned to, and live in, a barracks for a week or more. Times changed. The name didn't."

"Odd, but interesting. Anyway, I'm eager to speak with this Nate Holt. Let's hope he can give us some sound advice."

"Don't count on it," Pete replied. "OK, let's go."

Trooper Holt met us in the lobby. He was tall, thin and probably in his late forties. He had a dead serious look on his face as he escorted us to his office. He didn't offer us coffee. I was all right with that. My nerves were already on edge.

"Thank you so much for agreeing to meet with us," I said as we settled ourselves in his office. "We truly appreciate it."

Holt responded with a nod. "No problem. But I'll let you know from the get-go that I'm only meeting with you because I owe Donnelly a favor. He's an up-front guy. He seems to think you've got something worth looking into. So please tell me what you've got." He folded his hands on the table in front of him.

Not an auspicious beginning, but I refused to let that get me down. We told him our theory in great detail.

He listened. He took notes. Finally, he looked up and said, "If I understand you folks correctly, what you're telling me is that this group of Irish thugs hires the Mullins brothers to dispose of personnel in insurance agencies throughout the state, then somehow manages to replace these deceased employees with people of their own. These folks then act as spies to search out policies covering expensive jewelry. They code this information into Irish hieroglyphics and pass it on to the Mullins brothers, who, in turn, burglarize these clients. They take only expensive diamonds, which they fence or sell somewhere. The profits from this are laundered through the Café Begorrah restaurant in Sharon, which, needless to say, is owned and operated by the Irish mob."

I grimaced. The trooper's summary, while accurate, somehow managed to make it all sound like the plot of a bad movie. Pete caught my eye and silently advised me to hold my tongue. Good idea.

"Have I got it right?" the trooper asked. He put down his notes and made eye contact with me. "The trouble is that, as fascinating as this all is, you don't have any real proof."

"What about the fingerprints on the stuffed dog Mullins mailed me? What about the guy who spooked me on the street? I have been threatened more than once," I said.

He nodded. "I can't argue with that. And we take these threats seriously. Listen, we'd love to get the goods on the Mullins brothers. They've been on our radar off and on for years. And, by the way, thanks for providing us with their current address. Unfortunately, as far as the rest of it goes, much of it is merely conjecture."

"But it all fits together," I said. "I'm positive we've got it right."

"I'm not saying I don't believe you," he said. "Donnelly trusts your instincts. I trust his. I will look into everything you've told me. I simply need a few concrete facts."

"That's all we can ask," Pete said.

I added, "Don't worry. I have every intention of providing you with all the facts you need." I almost added "or die trying" but thought better of it. No point tempting fate.

"Whoa there," Holt said. "Leave the investigating up to us. It's our job. And we don't want anybody getting hurt."

It was my job as well, but I chose not to point that out. Besides, I planned to be very, very careful.

Pete and I said good-bye in the parking lot. "Good luck with your new client," I told him. "I hope your meeting goes well."

"And you be careful. Please, Ames, don't take any chances today. Don't do anything rash without at least running it by me."

"Duly noted." I stood on my tiptoes to kiss him good-bye.

"And call me if anything comes up."

"Will do." And I wished with all my heart that something would indeed come up.

Chapter 32

I dialed Peggy at the office before leaving the parking lot, then put my phone on speaker before driving off.

"Good morning to you," she said. Peggy was always gloriously cheerful in the morning. Most of the time, I liked that. Today, not so much. I was bummed out after the meeting with Trooper Holt. Also unsure how I was going to get the evidence I needed.

"Just touching base," I told her. "I should get to the office before lunch. I need to pick Sam up at Pete's and bring him back to my apartment. I'll be in after that. Is there anything happening that I should know about?"

"Not yet. But hope continues to spring eternal," she laughed.

"If you say so. Listen, can you please set up a meeting with you, Tiffany, George and, hopefully, Mark for some time this afternoon? I need to fill you all in on where we stand. And if we brainstorm, maybe we'll come up with some new, helpful angle. If not, at least George won't be able to say I'm not keeping him in the loop."

"Gotcha," she said. "Give Sam a hug for me. See you later."

I ended the call and headed off to Pete's to pick up Sam. I was more than a little nervous doing so. After all, the Mullins Brothers knew where Pete lived, having recently burglarized his house. I needed to grab my dog and get the hell away from Massapoag Junction fast. No sense putting either Sam or myself in danger—again.

I decided it'd be good to pay attention to where I was going. I wasn't all that familiar with the local roads and didn't want to get lost on my way to Pete's. I cursed myself for not setting the GPS. It was too late now. There was no place to pull over and rectify that. I moved into the right-hand lane, slowed to 25 miles an hour, and watched for my turn.

The driver behind me apparently wanted to go faster than 25. I sent him a silent message: *Back off, Buddy. You can always pass me!*

Rather than do so, he inched his car ever closer to my rear bumper. I tapped the brakes to warn him off. He beeped his horn and made an angry fist at me. I turned slightly and waved at him by way of apology. He remained perilously close to my Mustang. Apology apparently not accepted. A glance in my rearview mirror revealed an angry sneer on his face. This guy wasn't about to let it go.

I increased my speed just enough to pull a little further ahead of him and get a good look at his car. It was a beat-up brown sedan of indeterminate age. I couldn't identify the make, nor could I get a look at the license plate. He was too close to me for that.

I spotted my turn up ahead but decided not to signal. Better to surprise the guy, then hit the gas and get the hell away from him. Turning and hitting the gas worked fine for me. Happily, I had also managed to surprise my pursuer. I took off with as much speed as I dared to risk on a side road. So far so good. I took another right turn and hoped for the best.

Then my hopes were dashed. The brown sedan reappeared in my rearview mirror, quite a way behind, but closing fast. It was obvious that this was more than just some crazy dude suffering from road rage. Whoever this guy was, he was out to get me. My gut suggested he might be a Mullins.

I needed a plan. Fast. I was almost at the left turn that would take me to Pete's street, but didn't dare go that way now. If I pulled up at Pete's house, with my pursuer on my trail, he could easily corner me there. There was no way I was going to let that happen. I continued driving straight ahead, and as fast as I dared. A minor flash of inspiration hit me, reminding me about the Target store Pete and I had visited the other day. It wasn't far away. There would be people there. I'd be safe. At least for a while. Until I figured out what to do next. It was worth a shot.

I spotted the Target up ahead and ran a red light into the parking lot. Parking as close to the door as possible, I jumped from my Mustang and made a mad dash for the door. Looking back as I entered the store, I spotted the guy's car pulling in not far from mine. Now was a good time to lose myself in the aisles of the store.

I grabbed a shopping cart and hot-footed it to the far end of the building, then inserted myself into a large display of ladies' underwear. Perhaps my pursuer would be too embarrassed to approach me while I was thumbing through bras and panties. Perhaps not. He walked straight by without seeing me at first, but then caught himself and turned into the lingerie department. I resorted to zig-zagging up and down the aisles and ended up in the bath accessories section. I grabbed a few bath towels for Pete and threw them into my cart, not daring to look behind me. I veered into the home décor department and snuck a look in a decorative mirror. And there he was, closing in on me and not even pretending to be subtle about it.

I sped away to the checkout area and planted myself at the end of the longest line. He wouldn't dare do anything to me in front of all those people. At least I hoped not.

The line at the register moved more quickly than I wanted it to. All too soon I found myself approaching the exit and wondering what the hell to do next. There was a Starbuck's concession area just before the exit that looked like my best option. And there was no line at the counter. I grabbed a quick cup of coffee and seated myself at a nearby table with my back to the wall. At least the creep wouldn't be able to sneak up on me.

I pulled out my phone and called State Trooper Holt, leaving a semi-desperate message on his voicemail. I said a quick prayer he'd listen to it soon. I sipped my coffee and looked around everywhere at once. An old man sat a few tables away from me, mesmerized by a solitaire game on his iPad. He wouldn't notice if I were in trouble. Two young girls sat down at the table next to me. They probably wouldn't be much help either. My pursuer suddenly appeared out of nowhere. I got a good look at his face. Droopy eyelid. No doubt in my mind. This was the creep who followed me that night in Cambridge. And probably killed Tom Foye as well. And he was walking toward me with a nasty smirk on his face.

I was trying to decide whether to wait things out and see what developed, run like hell and hope for the best or confront the guy and create a public scene. I was weighing these options when a voice called out, "Hey, Mullins!" and a tall thin man dressed in ill-fitting camo pants and a dirty sweatshirt approached. "How are you doing, Mike?" he asked. "Haven't seen you in ages. Where have you been keeping yourself?"

Mullins looked uncomfortable, but there was no easy way he could ignore the guy.

This was my big chance to get away, not to mention my only one. I grabbed my bags and ran through the exit and to my Mustang. As I slammed the door and turned the key, I saw Mike Mullins emerge from Target and scan the lot for my car. I sped off and tried to disappear before he could catch up with me.

That worked fine for a few minutes. Mullins was nowhere to be seen in my rearview mirror. I dutifully hit the brakes at a four-way stop, then lost all hope as a funeral procession emerged from a side street, forcing me to wait. I checked the rearview mirror again. Mullins had reappeared and was closing in on me. Without hesitation, I turned on my headlights and flasher and insinuated my car into the funeral procession.

The mourner I had just cut off leaned on his horn and shook his fist at me. I didn't care.

I grabbed my phone out of my bag. The procession was moving just slowly enough that I felt it would be all right to place a call or two. The cop directing traffic at the intersection thought otherwise. As I was dialing Holt's number, the officer rapped on my windshield and shouted, "Put the phone down, Lady." That startled me just enough that I dropped the phone onto the passenger side floor. Not good. I needed help. And I needed it now.

I hit my brake and lowered my window. "Officer, I need help," I said.

That got his attention. "What's up?" he asked.

Before I could answer, his shoulder microphone squawked at him. "Hold on a minute, Lady." He leaned his head toward the microphone and listened for a moment. "I've got an emergency here," he said. "Pull over and I'll help you as soon as I can."

I was about to follow his instructions when the angry mourner behind me leaned on his horn. Seeing no safe place to turn over, I made a snap decision to remain with the funeral procession. At least that would keep me safe for a while. I stayed with them all the way to the cemetery on East Street in Sharon. I recognized the area. Pete's house was just a mile or so from the other end of that road. I remained in my car as the mourners stood at the grave for their final farewell. This won me a few odd looks from the mourners. I didn't care. It provided me with a few moments respite, a chance to call for help. I tried Holt again. Left another voicemail. Then I dialed Pete's cell. *Damn!* That call went straight to voicemail as well.

"Pete. It's me. And I'm in big trouble. Michael Mullins is after me. He followed me from the state police building all the way to Target. I had a hard time getting away. I'll tell you all about that later. Right now I'm in the middle of a funeral procession at the cemetery on East Street. And I can see Mullins's car waiting by the entrance. There's no way I can get away from him when I leave here. I'm going to stick with the funeral as long as I can. Then I'll try to head up East Street to Bay Road. Send help. Fast. Please."

The mourners returned to their cars and began driving out of the cemetery. The funeral director halted the traffic in both directions on East street so the procession could turn left. Mullins was forced to wait until they passed. I took advantage of this opportunity to turn right and head for Pete's house as fast as I could drive. If I could get to the end of East Street while the traffic was still stopped, I might just have a chance of losing my tail.

My phone rang. *Thank God!* Not Holt, though. Pete.

"Amy, are you all right? Where are you?"

"I'm safe for the moment," I said. "On my way up East Street heading to Bay Road. From there, I'm not sure what I'll do. I've left a message for Holt. Let's hope that he gets it soon. And that he gets here fast."

"Head for my place," Pete said. "I'll phone the local police and have them meet you there. I'm on my way there as well, and not too far behind you. I'm almost to Lake Massapoag. Do you still have that knife that you used to keep in the car?"

"Sure do. Tucked right into the pocket of my door. Thanks for reminding me." I reached down and grabbed the knife. It was only a six-inch blade. Nothing lethal. Still, it was better than nothing at the moment.

"Hang in there, Ames," Pete said. "It's going to be all right."

I was almost beginning to believe him, until I looked at the road ahead. "Holy shit, Pete! This is bad. There's a truck up ahead blocking the road at the fork. I can't stay on East Street. I have to turn onto Mountain Road. Now what do I do?"

"You'll have to take Mountain Road. It'll get you to Bay Road and ..."

And that's all I heard. My phone was dead. My GPS had cut out as well. Pete's neighbor was right. This road was a dead zone. I tried not to let this phase me as I continued up the road, ever-hopeful for the best. It appeared to be fine for the first mile or so—a decent road, a few scattered houses, a school. And then everything went to Hell fast. The road ahead was unpaved and rutted. And there were no more houses. Just woods on both sides of the road. Pete's neighbor wasn't kidding. Yet I had no choice but to forge on.

And then I couldn't. A white mini-van was parked cross-wise on the road ahead, leaving no way to get around it. And Mullins was fast approaching from behind. Now what?

I took a few deep breaths, steeled myself and did the only thing I could think of. I floored the gas pedal and rammed my Mustang into the rear passenger side of the mini-van. The van lurched under the impact. Unfortunately, there still wasn't room for me to get around it. My Mustang and I had survived the crash intact, but Mullins was still hot on my tail. Not good.

And then it got worse. I was backing up for a second assault on the van when an unpleasant-looking man got out of it, with gun in hand, aimed at me. He began to walk my way. I dropped my knife onto the seat beside me. No sense bringing it to a gunfight. My only option now was to run the guy down.

As I was about to hit the gas pedal, my Mustang was thrust forward to the shrieking sound of metal on metal. Mullins' car had bashed into my rear end. A moment later I felt a second impact as Mullins hit me a second time. My head smashed into the steering wheel.

Apparently I blacked out at that point.

When I came to, I had a massive headache. There was chaos all around me. Uniformed cops were everywhere, both Sharon police and state troopers. There was an ambulance as well, which was probably a good thing. I watched as state troopers wrestled Mullins to the ground while local police hand-cuffed the driver of the minivan. And Pete was there, frantically trying to open my car door. I smiled through my tears as he pulled me out of my car—and into his arms.

Chapter 33

Pete held me tightly. "It's all right now, Ames. You're safe. You're going to be fine."

I wiped away my tears with shaking hands. I'd be damned if I'd let the Mullins brothers see me cry.

Two EMTs joined us by my car. One of them said, "We need to check you out, Ma'am. And transport you if necessary."

"Not necessary," I said. "Just a little bump on the head. I'll be fine." *And I have things to do which can't wait.*

He checked my vital signs and my head, then frowned. "Doesn't look so little to me. And you did lose consciousness. That's nothing to take lightly."

I shook my head. "I get what you're saying, but I'm all right for now. If any problems crop up, I'll deal with them later."

Pete broke in, "I think you should listen to the man, Ames. He's the professional. And you're looking pretty shaky at the moment. Lord knows what damage that bang to your head may have done."

He was right, of course. My head was killing me.

"Listen to your friend, Ma'am," the EMT said. "Please come with us now."

I stood my ground. "Now is not a good time. I promise you that if my head doesn't stop hurting, or if I notice any signs of a possible concussion, I will go to the ER."

The EMT shook his head. "Do you know the signs of a possible concussion?"

I didn't even try to answer that.

"I promise you I will get her to the ER later today," Pete said. "After we get a few things sorted out here. How's that?"

The EMT frowned as he documented the incident then reluctantly went on his way.

A state trooper approached us, along with a local cop. "How are you doing, Ma'am?" the trooper asked.

"I'm fine" I lied. "How did you get here so fast?"

"I believe you can thank your boyfriend for that."

I turned to Pete.

He said, "As soon as your call dropped off, I called the local cops and let them know what was happening. They said they'd get here ASAP and would also notify Holt of the situation."

The local officer spoke up. "We were up the street working a construction detail on Bay Road. Your boyfriend reached you just before we did and decided to take matters into his own hands. He plowed his fancy new BMW into the Mullins car behind you. Officially, we don't condone, or advise, this type of maneuver. In this particular case, however, it appears to have been quite effective. Too bad about your car though. We've got a couple of tow trucks on their way. They should be here any time now."

I smiled up at Pete. "My hero. How bad is your car?"

He shook his head. "Don't worry about that. You're more important. It's easy to replace a car. I could never replace you."

The local cop smiled and resumed his narrative. "The state troopers arrived a few minutes later, much to the chagrin of the Mullins family."

Despite what I had told the EMTs, my brain was rather fuzzy. "So what exactly happened here?"

The trooper wrinkled his brow, then said, "As near as we can figure out, the Mullins brothers set a trap for you. There are three of them, you know. Michael, Seamus and Joe. One of them blocked the way on East Street, forcing you onto Mountain Road. A second brother entered Mountain Road from the other end. Your pursuer prevented you from backing up."

Good lord. Did they manage to do all that while I was at the cemetery?

The trooper continued, "And there you were. No way out. It's a good thing your boyfriend arrived when he did."

Amen to that!

Two tow trucks arrived on the scene. Pete and I watched in silence as both of our cars were spirited away. I shed a tear for my Mustang. I really loved that car. "You do realize that we have no way to get anywhere at the moment?" I said to Pete.

Officer Holt said, "Not to worry about that. I can give you a lift."

"Where to?" I asked.

Holt thought for a moment, then replied, "Back to the barracks to debrief both of you. We're going to need complete statements."

"Any possibility we could put that off until later?" Pete asked. "I don't believe Amy is at her best right now. I believe I should get her to the hospital now. Then once she's settled, I'll get a cab, or an Uber, or whatever, and go find myself a rental car then meet you back at your barracks."

"I guess that'd be all right," Holt said. "It's too bad the ambulance is gone. I can drop you folks at the ER. You'll probably have a better chance at being seen quickly if you arrive in a squad car. But you'll have to work things out on your own from there." He surveyed the madness around him. "I believe these folks can deal with this scene without my assistance. There are enough of my colleagues around to do a thorough job. Shall we go?"

The three of us piled into the trooper's car and off we went.

At the entrance to the ER, Holt said to Pete, "Let's not worry about you and I talking this afternoon. You've got more important things on your mind at the moment. How about the two of you, the Sharon cops and I get together in Foxboro tomorrow morning at 9:00?"

"Sure thing," I said. "I should be thinking much clearer then. I'm definitely not at my best at the moment."

Pete nodded. "I can certainly be there," he said. "I'm not so sure about Amy. We may need to do without her for a day or so, until I'm sure she's all right."

The trooper nodded. "Can do. We don't want the lady taking any more chances."

"Do you know if there's a car rental business somewhere close?" Pete asked.

Holt pursed his lips. "There is a place on Route 1. It should be easy enough for you to find. Take care of yourself," he said to me, then turned to Pete. "Let's see if we can wrap this up tomorrow morning."

Chapter 34

State Trooper Holt was right about the emergency room. The ER employees saw the squad car at the door and took me right away. We got a few dirty looks from some people in the waiting room, but my head was hurting so badly by then that I truly didn't care. I was feeling wobbly and was eager to lie down—anywhere nearby.

Pete stayed with me while I had my head examined—literally. If I had felt better, I would have made a joke about that. Sadly, this was not the time. All I wanted was to go to sleep and remain that way for a long time.

I got my wish.

I opened my eyes to find myself in a hospital gown with the room spinning around and Pete spinning above me with a look of concern.

"Welcome back," he said.

I tried to smile. It didn't work. "What time is it?"

"Late afternoon. Nearly 5:00."

"Have I been out all this time?"

He took my hand. "So they tell me. How do you feel?"

"Like I nearly got my head bashed in. Also pretty sure I'll topple over if I try to sit up."

"From what they told me at the nurses' station, you're likely to feel like that for a while. You have a concussion. It's relatively mild, but you still don't want to mess with it. And you're likely to have some vertigo."

"Vertigo, huh? Is that why the entire world is spinning at the moment?" I asked.

"So they tell me," he said.

"Well, let me tell you something as well ... it sucks."

That got me a small smile.

"Apparently that could last for a while," he added.

"That's not what I wanted to hear," I said.

"I know. And there's something else you won't want to hear either."

"I'm listening."

He hesitated, and looked everywhere except at me. That was not a good sign.

"Out with it, Pete. What is it?"

"They're going to keep you here overnight. For observation. Just to be safe."

That news brought a scowl to my face. "No! Is that really necessary? How am I supposed to wrap up this case and see to it that the Mullins brothers and their associates are locked up for a long time? I can't do any of that just lying around here."

He patted my cheek. "You have to take care of yourself, Ames. You gave us all a bad scare."

No point in arguing. Time to move on. "So what have you been up to these last few hours?"

"I spent a little time with the police."

"Sharon or State Police? Or both?"

"Sharon. I told them everything I could, which wasn't all that much. And I'm meeting with Holt first thing tomorrow. Everybody is hoping to speak with you as soon as you're up to it."

"I'll be up to it in no time, concussion or not. Don't worry about that," I told him. And I would find a way to see that I was.

Pete rolled his eyes. "I'm sure you will. By the way, I called Peggy. Gave her all the gory details. She says don't worry. She'll hold down the fort until you're feeling better. She also said don't hurry. Take it easy for a while."

"I'm sure she'll love being in charge."

"Also," Pete added, "Sam wanted me to give you his love."

"Oh, wow! Poor Sam. Is he all right?"

"He's fine," Pete said. "It's a good thing you hadn't left him in Cambridge. He and I had some lunch together, and a nice chat. When I left, he was in my back yard giving the ducks a hard time."

That made me smile. "I'm so glad that yard is fenced. Sam sure does love it there."

A young blond woman wearing bright pink scrubs and a serious look on her face appeared at the door. "Sorry to interrupt, folks. I have to check my patient's vitals. It'll only take a few minutes."

Pete stepped outside while the nurse did her thing.

"How am I doing?" I asked her.

"Well enough." She smiled. "You'll be out of here by tomorrow morning. But bear in mind that even a mild concussion is nothing to take lightly. Your head will hurt for a while, possibly several days. And you're likely to be unsteady on your feet. You need to take it easy. And get back in here ASAP if any of your symptoms get worse."

Pete returned with a cup of coffee and a donut in his hands. The thought of either of them turned my stomach. I forced myself to concentrate on other things. "What about our cars?"

"They're both total losses from what I could see. But we can deal with that later. I got a rental car for now," he said.

"Just one?"

"One's all we need for the moment. Once you're up to it, we can go car shopping together."

"I want a red car this time," I told him.

"You do? Why red?"

"Red cars go faster."

He chuckled. "I'm guessing your mother told you that."

"She did. She also said you can run faster in red shoes. I haven't tested that theory yet," I said. "Sounds like you've had a busy afternoon while I've just been hanging around doing nothing."

"I also threw in some laundry," he told me.

"Laundry?" I said. That seemed an odd thing to do under the circumstances.

"I wanted to make sure you'd have some clean clothes to leave here in tomorrow."

That made me smile. "You do think of everything, don't you?"

"I try."

And I was glad he did. That thought hit me like a bolt of lightning. As hard as I tried to be strong and independent, I didn't know what I'd do without Pete. I had come to rely on him for an increasingly large number of things. And that was OK with me—for the most part.

He stood to leave. "I better go now. See you in the morning."

I lay there awake thinking how lucky I was to have a guy like Pete. And making mental notes on what I needed to do to close out my investigation.

Chapter 35

I felt better the next morning. Not 100%, but I was getting close to 75% or so. The doctor declared me free to go and advised lots of rest. That sounded good to me. Pete arrived with clean clothes, and a cane to keep me from falling. "I didn't think you'd want a walker," he said.

He was right about that.

When I was dressed and ready to go, I realized the nurse hadn't been kidding. I had a killer headache and was more than a little unsteady walking. Pete held onto my arm and escorted me out to his rented SUV.

We hit traffic on the way to Foxboro and were the last to arrive at Trooper Holt's office. One other state trooper was there, as well as two Sharon cops, one male, one female. I may have recognized them from the debacle on Mountain Road, but I couldn't be sure. I hadn't been at my best at that time.

"Good morning, folks," Holt said. He flashed me a small smile. "Ms. Lynch, I'm happy to tell you we now have all the proof we need." He ushered us into a utilitarian conference room devoid of any charm or warmth. A pitcher of ice water sat on the table, as did a carafe of coffee. Neither one called out to me. There were still a few knots left in my stomach.

"Let me introduce you to State Trooper Frank Andrews and Officers Eleanor Dunne and Patrick Bates from the Sharon Police," Holt said. "Officers, this is Amy Lynch from New England Casualty and Indemnity and Attorney Peter Devereau."

We all acknowledged each other, murmuring greetings.

"How are you doing this morning, Ms. Lynch?" Holt asked.

"Getting better all the time," I told him, willing myself to make it so. "I'm tougher than I look."

Holt smiled. "That's what I heard from my buddy Frank Donnelly. He told me you're a very determined woman, and that your instincts are often right on target. He asked me to give you his best."

That was nice to know.

"A lot has happened since we saw you yesterday," Holt continued. "I believe you'll find it interesting."

Pete and I made ourselves as comfortable as we could in the small meeting room, eager to hear what Holt had to say.

He smiled. "First of all, thanks for bringing this diamond enterprise to our attention. With the geographically diverse locations involved here, odds are it never would have shown up on our radar otherwise. New England Casualty and Indemnity appears to have a well-run claims department." He consulted some notes on the table in front of him. "Based on Mr. Devereau's suggestion, Trooper Andrews took a drive to Hingham yesterday afternoon and had a long talk with Moira Delaney at the Zempke Agency. I'll let Frank tell you the rest."

"Moira was a fountain of information," Frank Andrews began. "And she was eager to speak with me. Almost relieved, I'd say. It seems that she was less than happy with her lot in life. She wanted out. She spilled her guts."

I was delighted to hear that, but not all that surprised. The dealings I had with Moira had given me that impression.

Andrews continued, "Moira and most of the other young female employees—what do you call them?"

"Customer Service Representatives," I told him. "Or CSRs."

He smiled. "Right. Thanks. So, the majority of these CSRs are illegals, brought to the U.S. by what can only be viewed as the Irish mob. Whitey Bulger's gift to the Commonwealth of Massachusetts. With a little help from Leo Maguire, who apparently owns both the Café Begorrah in Sharon and the Insurance Personnel business in Boston, these ladies came over here on tourist visas. Rather than the high-paying jobs they were promised, along with citizenship papers, they were forced into what can only be described as involuntary servitude. Then they quickly disappeared into the woodwork. They were tattooed on the arms or legs, to indicate that they belonged to Maguire, in that crazy Irish language. I'm not sure how to pronounce it."

"It's pronounced Ohm," I said.

Andrews rolled his eyes. "If you say so. Sure doesn't look like that. Anyway, they all began as waitresses at the Irish restaurant while they studied for their insurance licenses. They also learned how to use Ogham. That's how they communicated with the mob."

"I've got to admit it was a clever scheme," Holt said.

"Then, according to Moira," Andrews continued, "when positions opened up in any insurance agencies, and the owner went to Insurance Personnel for a replacement, Maguire placed these ladies there. Once ensconced in their jobs, their mission was to retrieve information on high-valued diamonds insured there and transmit this information to Maguire, in Ogham, of course. This all worked pretty well, as you can see by the extent of burglaries spread throughout the state."

"Did Moira tell you how these employment positions opened up?" I asked.

Andrews frowned, "She didn't have too many details, but the general idea was that the CSRs they were replacing had met with some kind of untimely demise. As often as not, their deaths appeared to be accidents. Moira says that wasn't so. It was all deliberate and extremely well-planned."

"Hell of a way to get a job," the female officer from Sharon said.

"That's for sure," Holt agreed. "When the new employees sent Maguire information on where the diamonds were, he'd contact the Mullins brothers, who would proceed to perpetrate the robbery."

I decided not to point out to him that it was considered burglary, not robbery. Nobody loves a know-it-all. "But that's not all the Mullins brothers did for Maguire, is it?"

"Sadly, no. The three of them played a major role in both ends of this scheme. They were responsible for disposing of agency employees by a variety of means in order to create a job vacancy. Their methods were varied, and occasionally bordered on the cruelly ingenious. Basically, these guys created the opportunity to obtain information, then acted on said information to steal the jewels. These jewels were then fenced or sold and the profits laundered through the restaurant in Sharon."

"Holy moly," the male contingent of the Sharon Police said. "That's nothing short of unbelievable. Diabolical, cruel and nearly impossible to detect. What a racket!"

I broke into a smile, delighted to learn that I had been right. "So what happens to the Mullins brothers now?" I asked Holt.

"They'll be charged with each and every offense we can make stick. The attempted murder of Ms. Lynch is a no-brainer. Most of the others murders would be difficult to prove. As would many of the thefts."

"It's too bad one of them wouldn't cut a deal and tell all," I suggested.

Holt's eyes grew wide. "How did you know about that? Donnelly told me he thought you were some kind of a witch."

"You mean one of them did?" I asked.

"Yes. Joseph, the youngest of the three. He decided he didn't want to spend the rest of his natural life in prison. He agreed to talk to us in exchange for a reduced sentence."

That was wonderful news.

"Seamus and Michael aren't taking it so well," Holt added. "We needed to place them in different facilities even while awaiting trial. Joseph insisted. He was convinced his brothers would kill him if the opportunity arose. I believe he was probably correct."

"What about Maguire?" I asked. "Has he been arrested as well?"

Holt shook his head. "I'm sorry to say the man is in the wind. I'm guessing that one of the Mullins boys tipped him off while they were laying the trap for you."

Bummer. "And the CSRs?" I continued. "What will happen to them?"

Holt frowned. "I have to say I feel bad for these poor women, but the law is the law. And the fact is that they were all complicit in a criminal enterprise. As they are also here illegally, they will be deported rather than prosecuted. It's a tough break for them, but it is better than doing jail time here."

I wasn't sure I agreed with him, but kept that thought to myself. "Even Moira?" I asked him. "After all, she helped you close the case."

"We are willing to cut a deal with her in exchange for her cooperation. Provided she is able to secure gainful employment within the next thirty days, she will be allowed to remain in this country, allotted a green card when appropriate and begin a path to citizenship."

That was a relief. "So all she needs is to find a job?" I asked.

Holt nodded.

"I'll give her one," Pete spoke up. "I could use some clerical help at my new office. And if she was bright enough to pass her insurance licensing exam, I'm sure she could master basic paralegal skills as well. The girl deserves a break."

All eyes turned in Pete's direction. Mine filled up with happy tears. "You're a good guy, Pete Devereau," I told him.

He shrugged it off. "I try."

After the meeting broke up, Pete and I stopped at a few car dealerships to see what was available. My heart wasn't in it yet, and I was tired and dizzy and my head hurt. Back at Pete's place, I crashed on the couch while Pete walked Sam. We had scotch and popcorn for dinner—the ultimate comfort meal in troubled times. Then I slept like the dead, which I very nearly had been. I'd deal with life in the morning.

Chapter 36

Pete needed to spend some time at his office on Sunday. I needed to spend more time on his couch. Sam was happy to keep me company. By evening, I tried to convince myself I felt much better. Still, I decided not to head home until morning.

Early Monday morning, Pete tried to convince me to stay at his place for a few more days. I refused. I needed to be home right now, in my own comfort zone. I'd find a way to make it work—a very slow, careful way.

Pete didn't argue with me. He disappeared into the bedroom for a few minutes and came out suitcase in hand. "I'm moving in with you for the foreseeable future," he announced. "Got to make sure you don't take any chances. I'll take the train back and forth to work for a while. At least until you can be trusted by yourself on those stairs. And Peggy can walk Sam when I'm not around. Any questions?"

I shook my head. "Sounds like you've got it all worked out just fine. And for once, I'm not going to say I'm fine on my own. I will accept your help for a while."

"Good to hear." He drove Sam and me back to Cambridge, giving me a stern lecture on taking it easy along the way. When we turned onto Cambridge Street, he asked, "Do you want me to drop you at your office so you can check in with folks? I'm sure Peggy could drive you home."

"No thanks. I'd like to stop at home first and get Sam settled. Besides, I want to try the stairs with you first, to see how I do."

"That'll mean an extra trip up and down the stairs, you know."

"I can deal with it," I told him. "I'm tougher than you think."

Climbing the stairs to my third-floor apartment was difficult. I doubted I could have done it without Pete's help, not to mention my new cane. The lack of balance was going to make my life difficult.

Pete had an appointment with a client. He drove me to my office on the way, walked me inside and arranged for Peggy to drive me home—very shortly. "And don't give her any arguments about that. Deal?"

"Deal."

"Good morning, Peggy," I said.

She gave me a stern look. "Good morning. Now, like Pete said, you only get a brief visit, then I'll drive you home."

"I wasn't necessarily expecting a hero's welcome," I said to her, "but I did hope you'd be glad to see me."

"I am. Very happy. But I'll be happier once you're back home and safely up those stairs."

I faked a frown.

She ignored it. "That was one heck of an accident you had. A concussion is nothing to take lightly, you know. You're lucky you weren't hurt worse."

"I know. So what's happening here?" I asked.

"Your claim is all set," she said. "Yours and Pete's. You should both have a check within a few days, so you can begin shopping for new cars."

That was good news.

Peggy wrinkled her brow. "Can I ask you something?"

"Sure."

"Was it very scary having that Mullins guy following you and boxing you in on that creepy road?"

"Scarier than I care to admit, but don't spread that around, please. I have a reputation to maintain," I said.

Peggy nodded. "Understood. And, by the way, many people here are simply marveling at your powers of deduction in unraveling the diamond theft scheme. It was all so complicated."

"You and Tiffany were a very big part of that effort. I couldn't have done it without the two of you. I'm pretty sure I couldn't de-code Ogham. Or translate Gaelic."

DEADLY DIAMONDS

She beamed at this praise.

"Where is Tiffany?" I asked.

"Home sick. Some kind of bug. Now go do what you feel you must. And make it quick."

"Yes, ma'am," I replied. "I think I'll check in with Mark now."

"I'll let him know you're on your way. You know how he hates surprises."

I took the elevator to the top floor. Mark met me at the door to his office. He greeted me with a big hug—highly atypical behavior for Mark. I rather liked it.

"It's good to see you in one piece, Amy," he said. "You gave us all a big scare, you know. Now, please, sit down before you fall down."

I smiled and sat. "I'm guessing you read my final report."

"Longest email I ever got," he laughed. "And thanks for being so detailed. You took a complicated situation and explained it clear as day. Nice job. I'm very impressed with how well you handled this case. It was a tricky one."

"Thanks. Don't forget that Peggy and Tiffany played a big part in sorting things out. Without their research, we never would have solved this case."

"Duly noted." He looked me straight in the eyes. "And bear in mind that without George bringing it to our attention in the first place, those thefts could have gone on indefinitely."

I suppressed a scowl. "Duly noted."

"Now go home and get some rest. Nancy will call you soon about getting together. In the meantime, I don't want to see your face again for at least a couple of days."

Mark was right. I was weary and wobbly and my head hurt like hell. I made my way to the elevator.

Peggy grinned as I returned downstairs. "A special delivery just arrived for you."

I peered into my office to see a dozen long-stem yellow roses in a vase. The card read: "Nice going, Amy. Congrats on a job well done. Regards, George."

I grinned as I realized that for the first time in ages, George hadn't called me Hotshot!

Peggy got me safely home and up the stairs. I spent the next several hours on the couch.

Pete showed up at my apartment just after 5:00. "Any idea where you'd like to have dinner?" he asked.

I gave this some thought. "How about Helmand? You know, that Afghani restaurant on First Street. I've heard some good things about it."

"Do you have any idea what Afghani cuisine consists of?" he asked.

"Actually, I do," I told him." I googled it this afternoon. There's a lot of lamb involved, prepared in a number of different ways. Other than that, beef or fish. Many dishes tend to include rice, onions and yogurt. Sounds pretty tasty to me. Besides, the restaurant is owned by Mahmood Karzai, the brother of the president of Afghanistan."

He grinned. "Why am I not surprised that you know such a thing? Sure. Let's check it out. I'll try anything at least once."

We drove to First Street, arriving early enough to have our pick of tables. A seat by the fireplace called out to me. I was seriously into cozy after my recent ordeal.

After we were seated, Pete said, "I don't know about you, but I could use a damn fine scotch again tonight. Maybe a double."

"Sounds good to me as well."

"Just be careful not to overdo it," he warned me. "You know you're still not quite yourself."

I sighed as loudly as I could. "I know I need a little help at the moment. But, you do know that I don't need a keeper, right?"

"And you do know that I worry about you, right? It is perfectly acceptable for you to let me take care of you once in a while."

"And you did a marvelous job of it the other day, absolutely heroic."

"It was my pleasure."

Once our scotch arrived, we fell silent and read the menu.

"What looks good to you?" Pete asked.

"Pretty much everything, but I think I'll go with the Koufta."

He consulted the menu again. "Spicy afghan meatballs, huh? Adventurous of you. I think I'll try this lamb dish called Chowpan. And how about we split an appetizer? This fried eggplant dish sounds tasty."

That decided, we lapsed into small talk, eager to avoid anything related to the past few days. Normal would be nice—at least for a while.

"Anything special doing at your new office?" I asked.

He shook his head. "Afraid not. I'm reviewing client files. So far everything looks just fine, though I need to put some serious time into it this week. And to begin training Moira."

"Is there anything else up for the week?"

Pete avoided eye contact and replied, "I think I'll pay a visit to the bank tomorrow. To put my mother's ring into a safe deposit box. I wouldn't want it to be stolen again."

Without even thinking, I blurted out, "Maybe you shouldn't do that. Not just yet."

His jaw fell open. "Really?"

"Really. At least we can talk about it."

About the Author

Like her heroine Amy Lynch, P.K. (Paula) Norton spent her career in the insurance industry. When she and her late husband Jack traveled throughout the U.S. and abroad, they entertained themselves by sitting in restaurants discussing interesting ways to kill people. As they plotted all manner of mysterious deaths and mayhem, the world of Amy Lynch was born. Paula's passions also become an integral part of her series—interests such as archaeology (Paula has lived in Paris and once worked at the archaeological dig described in *Dead Drop*), spies (Paula was a card-carrying member of the Association of Former Intelligence Officers), Paris, Key West, and fencing. *Deadly Diamonds* is the fifth book of the Amy Lynch Investigation series.

When she is not plotting or writing, Paula is, well, plotting and writing. She is a member of Sisters in Crime, the Cape Cod Writers Association, and the Rhode Island Authors Association.

Paula resides in Easton, Massachusetts.

Made in the USA
Middletown, DE
14 October 2021